EARTH
ENCOUNTERS
THE ARRIVAL

SPECIAL THANKS TO

JOHN TEMPLE

A PROUD AND

GOOD MAN WHO SEES

ALL CHALLENGES

AND DIFFICULT

SITUATIONS IN LIFE

AS A GLASS HALF FULL

RAISE A GLASS!

EARTH ENCOUNTERS: THE ARRIVAL
WRITTEN AND CREATED BY
L. T . WALKER
BASED ON THE SOCIALLY CONSCIOUS BOARD GAME
EARTH ENCOUNTERS

www.earthencounters.us

Art by
TONI SHARK

L. T . WALKER INC>

DEDICATIONS

JASON WALTER TEMPLE,

THE BELOVED SON OF MY BEST FRIEND, JOHN TEMPLE.

JASON WAS A BRIGHT LIGHT

THAT WAS EXTINGUISHED MUCH TOO SOON.

HIS PASSING LEFT A VOID IN THE HEARTS

OF EVERYONE WHO KNEW HIM.

R.I.P. JASON

09/12/1982 – 08/16/2021

TO MY FAMILY –

JOYCE, TAYLOR, COREY, JORDAN

LOVE, DAD

IF YOU WERE SEARCHING FOR HEROES TO SAVE EARTH,

WHERE WOULD YOU LOOK?

SOME STORIES MUST BE TOLD IN A DIFFERENT WAY

BECAUSE

AMERICA'S PAST, PRESENT AND FUTURE DEMAND IT.

IT STARTS.

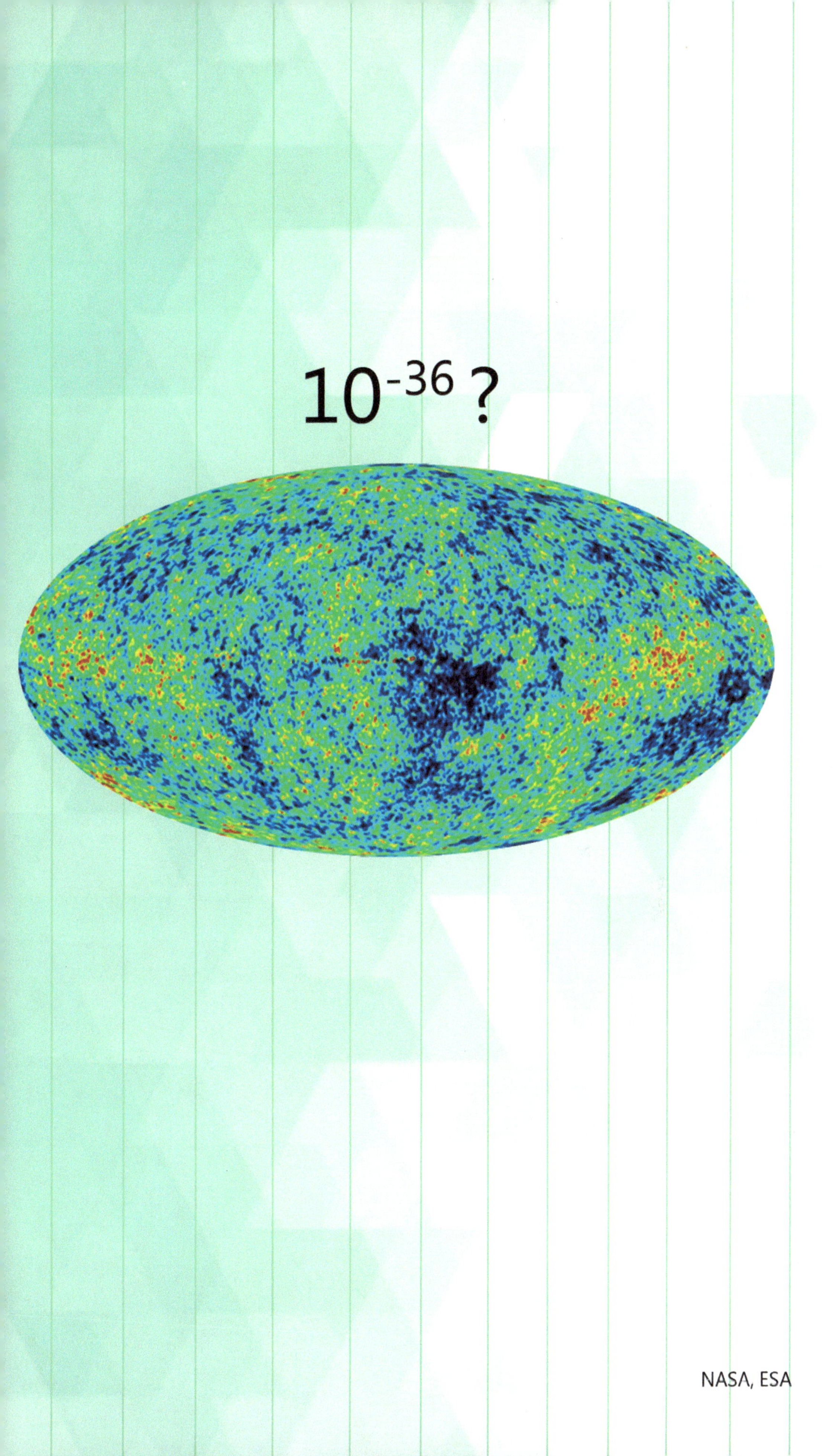

10^{-36} ?
NASA, ESA

"WE ARE CHILDREN OF LIGHT"
NASA, ESA, CSA, and STScI

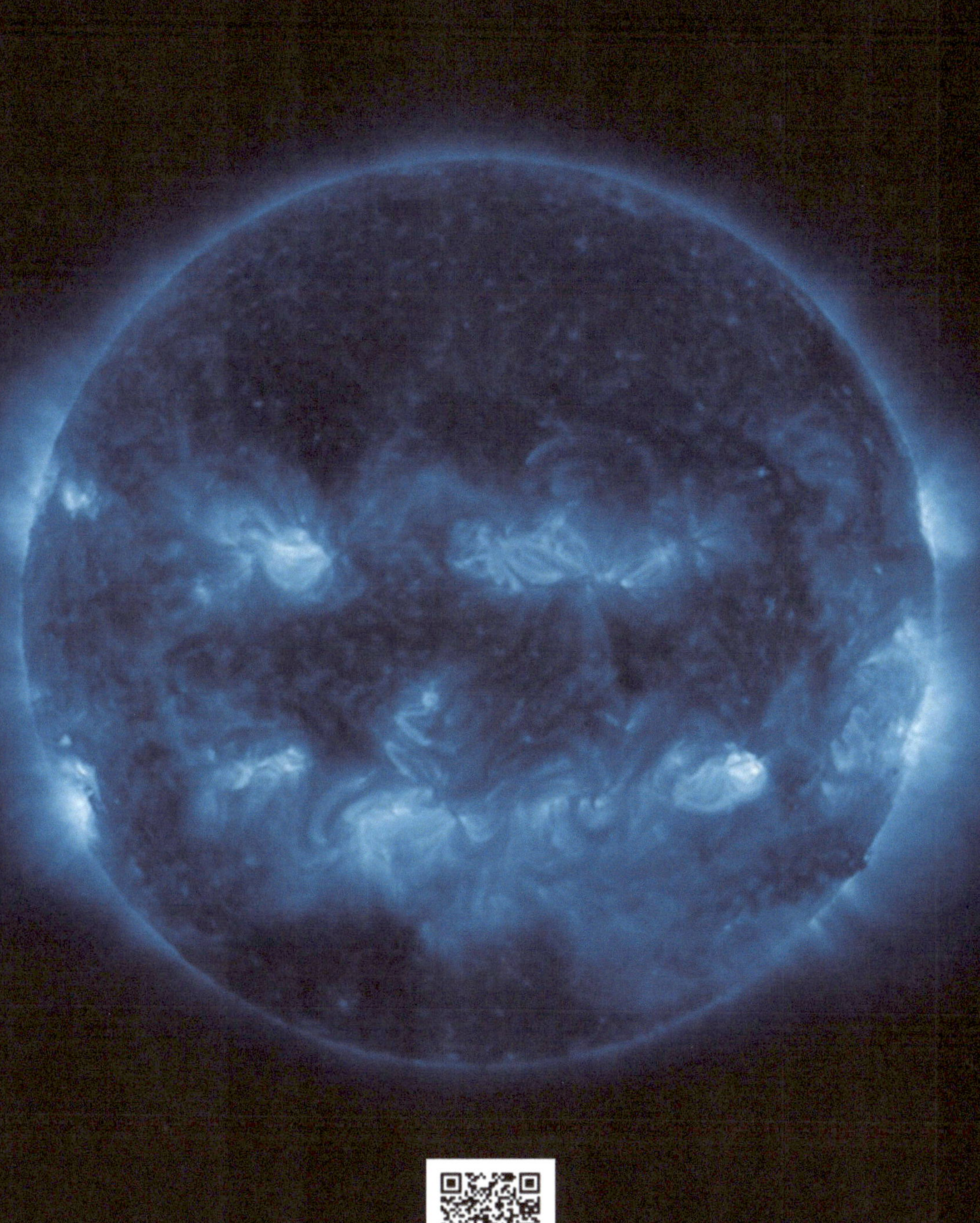

FIND EARTH – PAUSE – REFLECT

NASA/SDO

EARTH
ENCOUNTERS
THE ARRIVAL

LATE 1850S :
ON A COLD
WINTER
MOONLIT
NIGHT
SOMEWHERE
BETWEEN
THE EASTERN
SHORE OF
MARYLAND AND
PHILADELPHIA
HARRIET
TUBMAN
WALKS
ALONE DOWN
A REMOTE
DIRT ROAD
TO RESCUE
MORE ENSLAVED
PEOPLE
TO LEAD
THEM
TO FREEDOM

SUDDENLY FROM BEHIND A SOFT LIGHT APPEARS UNLIKE ANYTHING HARRIET HAS EVER EXPERIENCED
SHE DOESN'T TURN TO SEE THE SOURCE INSTEAD SHE LOOKS STRAIGHT AHEAD DETERMINED BUT UNAFRAID
TELE PATHICALLY HARRIET HEARS..
WE ARE HONORED TO BE IN YOUR PRESENCE
PLEASE CALL US...
"FRIENDS"
THE FRIENDS SHOW HARRIET AMERICA 30,000 YEARS IN THE FUTURE IN LESS THAN ONE SECOND
WITHOUT SPEAKING, THE FRIENDS AND HARRIET AGREE TO A NEW CHALLENGE
SHE AND OTHERS WILL LEAD AMERICA 30,000 YEARS IN THE FUTURE ONCE THEY COMPLETE THEIR CURRENT FIGHT FOR FREEDOM
AND THEIR LIFE ON EARTH COMES TO AN END
HARRIET TUBMAN CONTINUES HER WALK ON THE REMOTE DIRT ROAD HOLDING A LONG RIFLE

Dinosaurs: Guardians of Earth's Past

Dinosaurs, the magnificent titans of prehistory, roamed the Earth for an astonishing span of over 160 million years. Their reign began roughly 230 million years ago in the Mesozoic Era and concluded around 65 million years ago. These creatures, ranging from the colossal and fearsome Tyrannosaurus rex to the gentle, long-necked Brachiosaurus, left an indelible mark on the history of our planet.

Dinosaurs inhabited every corner of the Earth, adapting to a multitude of environments. Their existence spanned three geological periods: the Triassic, Jurassic, and Cretaceous. During these eras, dinosaurs evolved into diverse species, each uniquely suited to their habitats. The Earth's climate, flora, and fauna were significantly shaped by their presence, influencing the development of ecosystems that supported life as we know it today.

The influence of dinosaurs on the history of Earth is profound. They were the dominant terrestrial vertebrates, and their interactions with the environment played a crucial role in shaping the planet's biodiversity. Dinosaurs were pivotal in the evolution of other species, including mammals and birds. In fact, many scientists believe that modern birds are the direct descendants of theropod dinosaurs, highlighting the enduring legacy of these ancient creatures.

The question of how dinosaurs became extinct has intrigued scientists for decades. The prevailing theory is that a cataclysmic event, likely an asteroid impact, led to their demise. Around 65 million years ago, a massive asteroid, estimated 10 kilometers in diameter, struck the Yucatán Peninsula in present-day Mexico. The impact created a crater known as the Chicxulub crater and released an unimaginable amount of energy. The resulting shockwaves, wildfires, and dust clouds drastically altered the Earth's climate.

This catastrophic event caused a rapid and dramatic environmental change, leading to the mass extinction of around 75% of all plant and animal species, including the non-avian dinosaurs. The sudden climate shift disrupted food chains and ecosystems, making it impossible for the dinosaurs to survive. This extinction event, known as the Cretaceous-Paleogene (K-Pg) extinction, paved the way for the rise of mammals and, eventually, the emergence of humans.

Dinosaurs and the many sea creatures that inhabited the earth with them may no longer rule the Earth, but their legacy lives on. They continue to captivate our imagination, inspire scientific discovery, and remind us of the ever-changing nature of life on our planet. Their story is a testament to the grandeur of evolution and the resilience of life in the face of unimaginable challenges.

They still rule among other stars. I know this to be true. I walk, fly, and swim with them. They were a gift to humans, debt repaid.

MR. D – EXODUS PROJECT - VICTORY

DAYLIGHT - EARTH UPPER CRETACEOUS PERIOD 66 MILLION YEARS AGO - A LAND THAT WILL EVENTUALLY BECOME AMERICA
A MUSCULAR MASKED FIGURE 6'5" "MR.D" IN HIS BLACK EXODUS SUIT AND PETITE 5' MASKED FIGURE "NEUTRINA" FEMALE BIO-TRI-ANDROID
DESCEND MORE THAN ONE HUNDRED FEET FROM THE CLOAKED TIMESHIP, SHADOW THEY APPEAR TO BE JUMPING FROM AN OPENING IN THE SKY
"NEUTRINA" -BIO-TRI ANDROID PETITE BUT POWERFULL VIRTUE
"MR.D" LEADER EXODUS PROJECT VICTORY
SSSSS
SSS
H
SYEEET
NEUTRINA - A GIFT TO M.O.M. FROM "FRIENDS"
HER PRIME DIRECTIVE PROTECT MR. D

NEUTRINA, FEMALE BIO-TRI - ANDROID - IT COMPRISES THREE FORGOTTEN GROUPS - YOUNG ASIAN, BLACK, AND NATIVE AMERICAN GIRLS SOLD INTO PROSTITUTION OR RAPED BY THOSE ENSLAVING AND ABUSING THEM DURING 19TH CENTURY AMERICA. THEY EXIST AS ONE AND IN THEIR ETHNICITIES, ABLE TO MERGE AND SEPARATE AT WILL. NEUTRINA IS A GIFT TO M.O.M. FROM THE FRIENDS, BEINGS FROM ONE MILLION YEARS INTO OUR FUTURE. ALTHOUGH NEUTRINA TAKES THE FORM OF A PETITE 5' HUMAN, SHE MAY BE THE MOST POWERFUL SUPERHERO ANDROID IN THE UNIVERSE. SHE POSSESSES KNOWLEDGE OF ALL HUMAN HISTORY.
MR. D AND NEUTRINA WALK ACROSS A GRASSY AREA SEPARATING A HEAVY FOREST FROM THE ROCKY SHORELINE OF A MASSIVE BODY OF WATER.
TRONA NEUTRINA - AFRICAN AMERICAN
TAU NEUTRINA - NATIVE AMERICAN
MU NEUTRINA - CHINESE AMERICAN
THEY STAND ON A HILL ABOVE THE ROCKY SHORELINE. NEUTRINA HAS OSCILLATED INTO THREE OF HER FOUR STATES GHOST IS THE FOURTH STATE OF NEUTRINA IT EXISTS BETWEEN "CHILDREN OF LIGHT" AND THE DARK UNIVERSE
IT HOLDS THE SECRET TO FASTER-THAN-LIGHT COMMUNICATION SPACE TRAVEL, AND TIME TRAVEL UTILIZING THE DARK MATTER WEB THAT BINDS ALL GALAXIES THE DARK MATTER WEB IS CALLED THE DARK HIGHWAY

As they watch, Hesperomis, 7-foot-long birds with sharp teeth, beach themselves on the beach, sliding on their bellies to mate. Predators attack several before making land in the water, including several menacing types of mosasaurs, including the Halisaurus. However, rarely this close to shore appears the king of the sea mosasaurs, the 50-foot-long Tylosaurus carrying in its mouth a 23-foot-long predator fish, the Xiphactinus.

AS MR. D, TRONA, TAU, AND MU NEUTRINA CONTINUE TO WATCH THE ONGOING DRAMA ON THE BEACH AND IN THE WATER, A LARGE HERD OF CARNIVOROUS DINOSAURS RAPIDLY APPROACHES THEM FROM THE FOREST. THE FOUR FIGURES IGNORE THEM AS THE BEASTS SLOWLY STALK THEM FROM BEHIND.

THE ALPHA T-REX AGGRESSIVELY LOWERS HIS HEAD A FEW FEET FROM THE GROUP AND ROARS.
RROR!!
ROOA
THE ALPHA T-REX AGGRESSIVELY STANDS DIRECTLY BEHIND MR.D, WITH ITS HEAD LOWERED TO BE JUST ABOVE HIM.
MR.D RAISES HIS ARM AND PETS THE BEAST WITHOUT TURNING.
HARD TO BELIEVE
ONE DAY THIS WILL BE KANSAS
WHILE IGNORING THE BEASTS, TRONA NEUTRINA TURNS TO MR.D, POINTING TOWARDS THE WATER.

THEY WALK AWAY FROM THE SEA THAT COVERS MUCH OF PRE-MIDDLE AMERICA BETWEEN MASSIVE NUMBERS OF PREDATOR AND NON-PREDATOR SPECIES; ALAMOSAURUS, PACHYCEPHALOSAURIA, AND VELOCIRAPTORS, FOLLOWED BY THE TWO MASSIVE T-REX. MASKS NOW COVER THE HEADS OF EACH NEUTRINA.
THREE NEUTRINA BECOME TWO
TWO NEUTRINA BECOME ONE
MR. D AND NEUTRINA SLOWLY RISE 100 FEET INTO WHAT APPEARS TO BE A CIRCULAR RIPPLE IN THE SKY AS THE DINOSAURS WATCH.

SUDDENLY, ANIMALS OVER LARGE SECTIONS OF LAND, AIR, AND WATER ARE STARTLED AS ENERGY BEAMS STRIKE THEM FROM UNSEEN TIMESHIPS IN EARTH ORBIT, TRANSPORTING THEM TO THE MOTHER TIMESHIP, ENCOUNTER.
ON LAND
SEA
AND AIR
SILENCE

IT STARTS

FROM ABOVE AND BEHIND, MR. D AND NEUTRINA STAND ON THE MASSIVE VIEWING DECK ABOARD A TIMESHIP IN LOW EARTH ORBIT WITH A PANORAMIC VIEW OF EARTH AS, IN THE DISTANCE, AN ENORMOUS BLAZING HOT METEOR IS ROARING INTO EARTH'S ATMOSPHERE FROM SPACE.

MR. D, THE EXODUS PROJECTS LEADER, UNDER MOTHERS OF MEN'S DIRECTION, M.O.M. STAR I, (LIBERARE, ET CUSTODIRE)- LIBERATE AND PROTECT.

EXODUS PROJECT - RESCUE INHABITED PLANETS FROM EXTINCTION DUE TO SOLAR FLARES, SOLAR SUPER STORMS, DEATH OF A SUN, ASTEROIDS, COMET COLLISIONS, SUPERNOVA, PULSARS, MAGNETARS, QUASARS, BLACK HOLE COLLISIONS, BINARY STAR COLLISIONS, GENOCIDE, POLLUTION, MORE.

THIRTY THOUSAND YEARS INTO EARTH'S FUTURE
IN A FAR-OFF GALAXY
A PEACEFUL SPECIES OF HIGH INTELLECT AND SOCIALIZATION FACES EXTINCTION.
THE LEADER AND LAST SURVIVOR OF A DANGEROUS INVISIBLE VIRUS-LIKE SPECIES WITH EXTRAORDINARY POWERS HAVE INVADED THIS WORLD. IT IS THE MICEOV. MR. D HAS LED HIS TEAM TO CAPTURE AND RID THE UNIVERSE OF THIS CREATURE.
AN INFECTED PET OR WILD ANIMAL CAN BECOME EITHER A CARRIER OR A BEAST.
ONCE A MEMBER OF AN INTELLIGENT SPECIES IS INFECTED, IT BECOMES ONE WITH THE MICROV WITH ITS VAST INTELLECT, STRENGTH, AND ABILITIES BEYOND IMAGINATION. THEY WILL LOOK THE SAME BUT ARE NOW A THREAT TO EVERYONE.
MILLIONS HAVE HIDDEN BENEATH THE PLANET'S SURFACE TO ESCAPE INFECTION. IT FEEDS ON THE KNOWLEDGE OF INTELLIGENT BEINGS.
IT PENETRATES THE VICTIM'S BRAIN, ENSLAVING THEM WHILE ABSORBING THEIR KNOWLEDGE.

THE PLANET LEADERS HAVE FLED TO A MASSIVE HALL TO ESCAPE THE PURSUING CREATURES. A FEMALE OF THE SPECIES, AND THEIR LEADER, ADDRESS THE GROUP.
OUR PETS AND WILD ANIMALS WERE A GIFT TO OUR LIVES. NOW, THEY ARE ATTACKING AND KILLING US! WE HAVE LOCATED THE SOURCE OF THIS INFECTION. BUT, WHATEVER IT IS, ITS POWERS ARE BEYOND OUR ABILITY TO DESTROY IT.

BANG BANG!!!!
I HAVE FAILED YOU. ALL IS LOST.
WE HAVE LOST THOUSANDS. SOON, IT WILL DISCOVER WHERE MILLIONS ARE HIDING UNDERGROUND.
I AM ORDERING AN IMMEDIATE EVACUATION TO TRIDON. WE WILL HONOR THOSE WE HAVE LOST BY FINDING A WAY TO TAKE BACK OUR WORLD AND DESTROY THE INVADER.
LOOK!
SHE HEARS A SCREAM FROM THE ENTIRE GATHERING.
THEY POINT TOWARD THE HIGH CEILING

MASKED MR. D AND NEUTRINA HOVER NEAR THE HIGH CEILING, EACH SURROUNDED BY A GLOWING LIGHT.
THEIR BODIES FIRE A BLINDING LIGHT, FILLING THE ROOM AS THE CROWD SCREAMS.
AAAAAHHHH!!
THE LEADERS HAVE DISAPPEARED, LEAVING THE ENTIRE HALL EMPTY, WITH ONLY THE CREATURES RETURNED TO THEIR ORIGINAL FORM AS HARMLESS ALIEN PETS.
PLOP

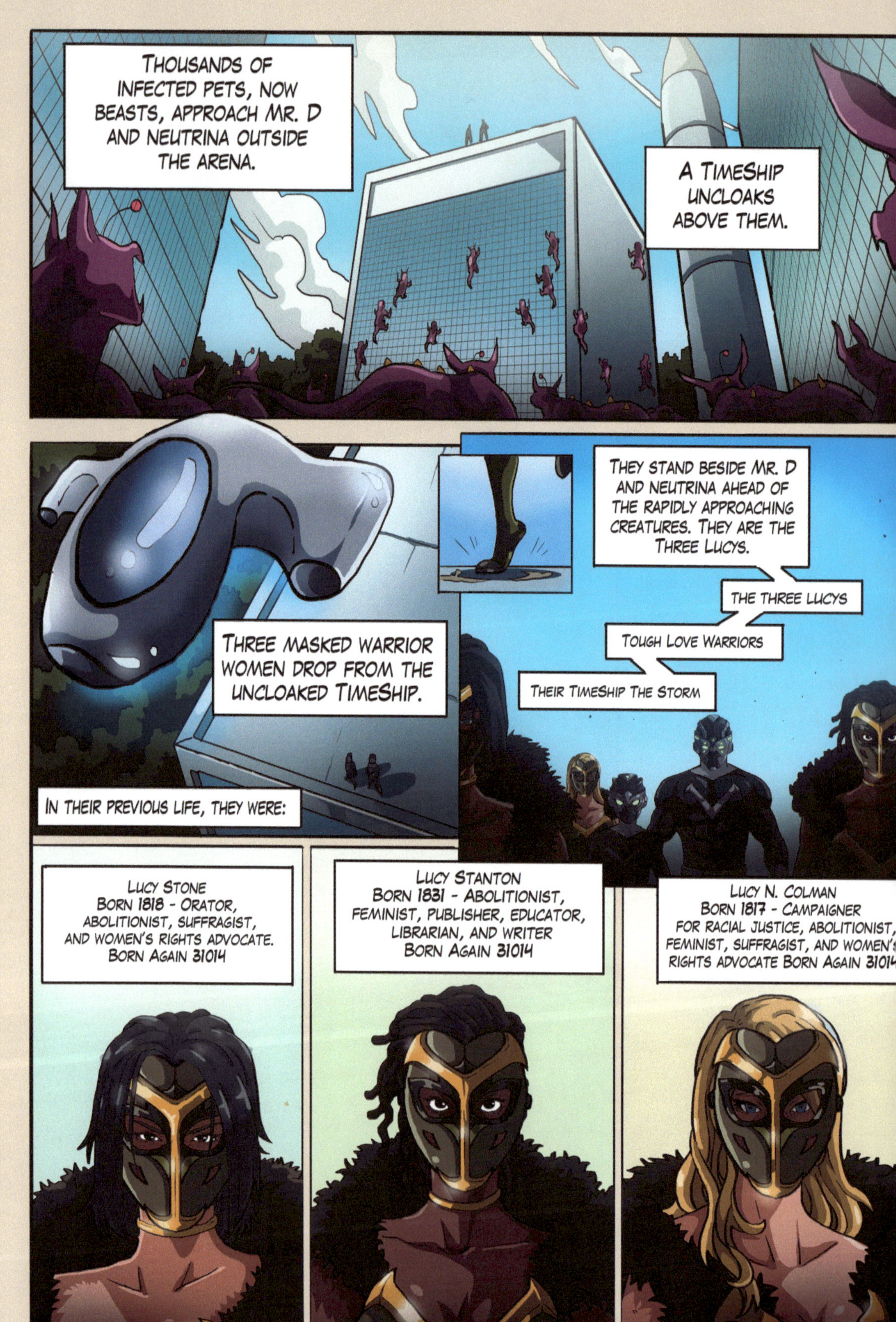

THOUSANDS OF INFECTED PETS, NOW BEASTS, APPROACH MR. D AND NEUTRINA OUTSIDE THE ARENA.
A TIMESHIP UNCLOAKS ABOVE THEM.
THREE MASKED WARRIOR WOMEN DROP FROM THE UNCLOAKED TIMESHIP.
THEY STAND BESIDE MR. D AND NEUTRINA AHEAD OF THE RAPIDLY APPROACHING CREATURES. THEY ARE THE THREE LUCYS.
THE THREE LUCYS
TOUGH LOVE WARRIORS
THEIR TIMESHIP THE STORM
IN THEIR PREVIOUS LIFE, THEY WERE:
LUCY STONE BORN 1818 - ORATOR, ABOLITIONIST, SUFFRAGIST, AND WOMEN'S RIGHTS ADVOCATE. BORN AGAIN 31014
LUCY STANTON BORN 1831 - ABOLITIONIST, FEMINIST, PUBLISHER, EDUCATOR, LIBRARIAN, AND WRITER BORN AGAIN 31014
LUCY N. COLMAN BORN 1817 - CAMPAIGNER FOR RACIAL JUSTICE, ABOLITIONIST, FEMINIST, SUFFRAGIST, AND WOMEN'S RIGHTS ADVOCATE BORN AGAIN 31014

THE LUCYS CREATE A FORCE FIELD BLOCKING THE CREATURES' ADVANCE AND PREVENTING THEIR ESCAPE.
MR. D FLIES THROUGH THE FORCE FIELD WHERE THE CREATURES ARE TRAPPED.
THOUSANDS OF SINGLE ENERGY BEAMS RAIN DOWN UPON THE TRAPPED BEASTS AND MR. D FROM CLOAKED TIMESHIPS IN LOW EARTH ORBIT.
THE CREATURES ARE SCATTERED ACROSS THE GROUND, GRADUALLY RETURNING TO THEIR NATURAL SHAPE. MR. D STANDS, HOLDING A CUTE PET THAT SEEMS HAPPY TO SEE HIM.

LOOKING TOWARDS SPACE, STILL MASKED, MR. D SENDS A TELEPATHIC COMMAND TO THOUSANDS OF. UNSEEN TIMESHIPS
ALL TEAMS. FIRE TO CONTAIN ON MY COORDINATES. NOW!
SUDDENLY, A MASSIVE DISTURBANCE OCCURS, CAUSING THE ATMOSPHERE TO VIBRATE AND EMIT AN EAR-SHATTERING SOUND. AS FAR AS THE EYE CAN SEE, IN THE SKY ARE THOUSANDS OF TIMESHIPS, EACH FIRING A SINGLE BEAM OF ENERGY TO A DISTANT LOCATION, STRIKING THE INVISIBLE CREATURE'S SHIP AS IT ATTEMPTS TO ESCAPE.

THE STORM APPROACHES THE 30' TALL INDESTRUCTIBLE CRYSTAL SHIP CONTAINING THE DEADLY MicroV. IT IS THE MONSTER'S SOURCE OF LIFE AND POWER, INCLUDING SPACE TRAVEL. THERE IS A SLIGHT MOVEMENT IN ITS CENTER.
THE MicroV IS CAPTURED.
TRIDON! HOW?
WE CAPTURED THE CREATURE. YOUR PEOPLE NEED YOU. IT'S TIME TO GO HOME.
SAFE TRAVELS HOME. GO WITH LOVE.
PLEASE ACCEPT THIS SYMBOL OF HOPE. IT WILL TELL OUR STORY. SHARE IT WITH YOUR PEOPLE. WEAR IT ON YOUR BODY.
BUT PLEASE CARRY IT IN YOUR HEART AND MIND. WE ARE ON A CRITICAL MISSION. WE INVITE YOU TO JOIN US WHEN YOU ARE READY
SUDDENLY, FROM ABOVE, THEY ARE STRUCK AGAIN BY A POWERFUL BLAST FROM TIMESHIP, STORM.

AMERICA - 30,000. YEARS IN THE FUTURE
DAYLIGHT
THREE MEMBERS OF M.O.M. ARRIVE FOR THEIR SCHEDULED HEADQUARTERS MEETING.
SUSAN LA FLESCHE- BORN 1865- FIRST FEMALE NATIVE AMERICAN TO EARN A MEDICAL DEGREE IN THE U.S BORN AGAIN - 30114
FRANCES ELLEN WATKINS HARPER- BORN 1825 - POET AND ONE OF THE FIRST BLACK WOMEN TO PUBLISH A NOVEL. BORN AGAIN - 30124
LUCRETIA MOTT BORN 1793 - ABOLITIONIST WOMEN'S RIGHTS ACTIVIST, SOCIAL REFORMER, AND FEMINIST. BORN AGAIN 30114
AS THEY WALK, THEY ARE STALKED FROM ALL SIDES BY SEVERAL LARGE PREDATORY CATS, A LION, LEOPARD, AND TIGER, RAPIDLY CLOSING IN ON THEIR PREY.
THEY SENSE SOMETHING LURKING IN THE TALL GRASS
THEY KNOW THE BUILDING IS TOO FAR AWAY.
TOO FAR! NO WAY! WE'RE GONNA MAKE IT!
IT'S YOUR FAULT, BOTH OF YOU. LET'S DO THIS!

HARRIET - HARRIET TUBMAN - LED MORE THAN 300 OTHER SLAVES TO FREEDOM. BORN AGAIN - 30014
MUMBET - ELIZABETH FREEMAN HER SUIT ENDED SLAVERY IN MASSACHUSETTS. BORN AGAIN - 30015
WIN - SARAH WINNEMUCCA ,NATIVE AMERICAN AUTHOR .ACTIVIST, AND EDUCATOR BORN AGAIN - 30015
TRUTH SOJOURNER TRUTH FAMOUS BLACK ABOLITIONIST. BORN AGAIN - 30015
HARRIET! LADIES!
WE SAW EVERYTHING.
GROW U WE'VE GO WORK TO DO!
MOTHERS OF MEN
E Pluribus Unu

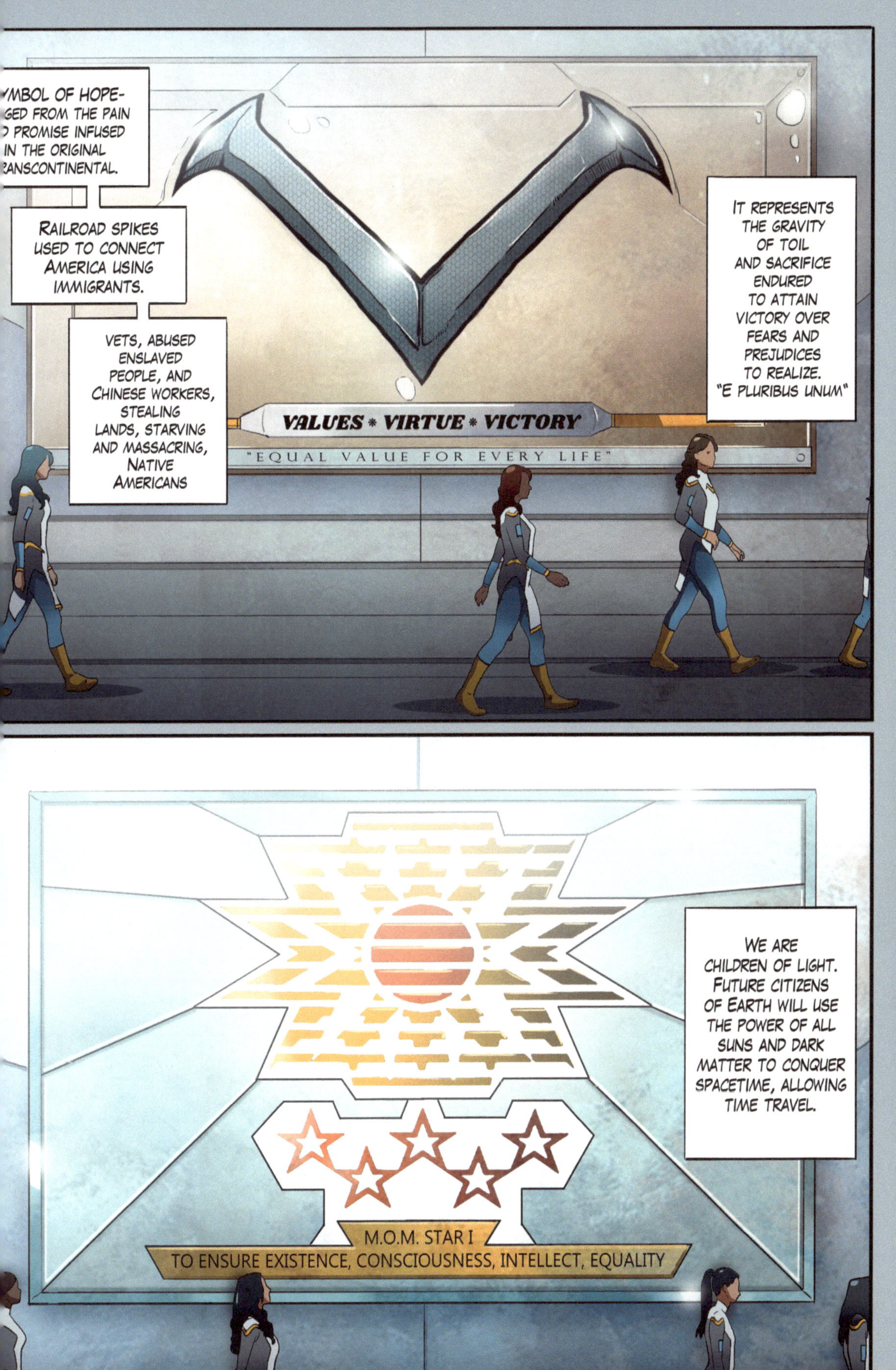
YMBOL OF HOPE-
GED FROM THE PAIN
D PROMISE INFUSED
IN THE ORIGINAL
RANSCONTINENTAL.

RAILROAD SPIKES
USED TO CONNECT
AMERICA USING
IMMIGRANTS.

VETS, ABUSED
ENSLAVED
PEOPLE, AND
CHINESE WORKERS,
STEALING
LANDS, STARVING
AND MASSACRING,
NATIVE
AMERICANS

IT REPRESENTS
THE GRAVITY
OF TOIL
AND SACRIFICE
ENDURED
TO ATTAIN
VICTORY OVER
FEARS AND
PREJUDICES
TO REALIZE.
"E PLURIBUS UNUM"

VALUES * VIRTUE * VICTORY
"EQUAL VALUE FOR EVERY LIFE"

WE ARE
CHILDREN OF LIGHT.
FUTURE CITIZENS
OF EARTH WILL USE
THE POWER OF ALL
SUNS AND DARK
MATTER TO CONQUER
SPACETIME, ALLOWING
TIME TRAVEL.

M.O.M. STAR I
TO ENSURE EXISTENCE, CONSCIOUSNESS, INTELLECT, EQUALITY

EARTH - 30,000 YEARS IN THE FUTURE
M.O.M. – MOTHERS of MEN
Leaders of what was once the United States of America, now "America."
America consists of five regions, each governed by M.O.M.
In 3050, our responses to a series of catastrophic events resulted in all 56 states voting to
dissolve their charter, ratify a new constitution, and approve the M.O.M. regional
structure and the new American flag. Our species has evolved exponentially since then.
Now, there is a shared vision of America. Finally, our values match the words in
AMERICA'S NEW LIVING CONSTITUTION
AND
EARTH IS A FOUNDING MEMBER OF THE UNIVERSE OF NATIONS TO DEFEAT
A CHALLENGE BEYOND COMPREHENSION
E PLURIBUS UNUM

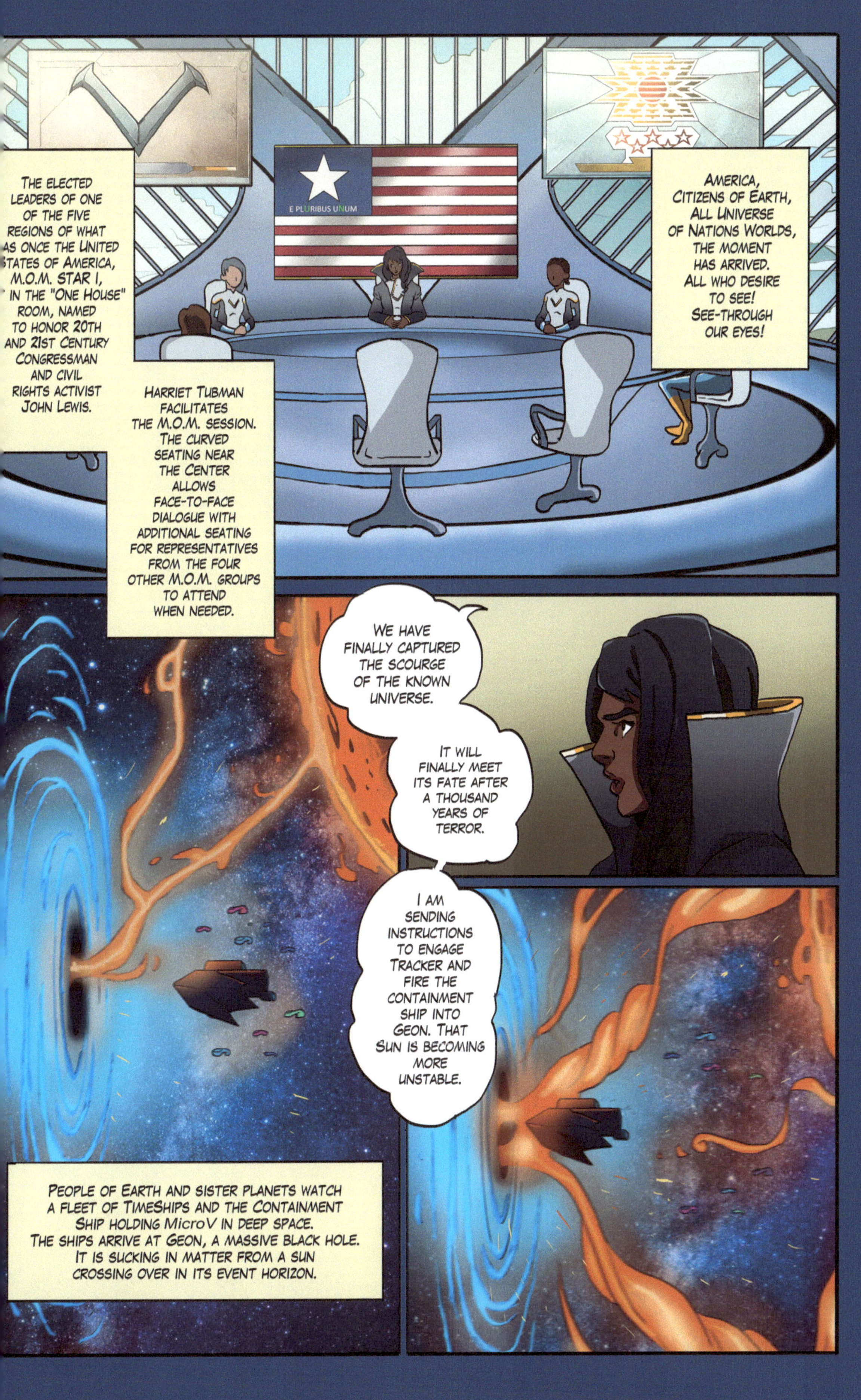

E PLURIBUS UNUM
The elected leaders of one of the five regions of what was once the United States of America, M.O.M. Star 1, in the "One House" room, named to honor 20th and 21st Century Congressman and civil rights activist John Lewis.
Harriet Tubman facilitates the M.O.M. session. The curved seating near the center allows face-to-face dialogue with additional seating for representatives from the four other M.O.M. groups to attend when needed.
America, citizens of Earth, all Universe of Nations worlds, the moment has arrived. All who desire to see! See-through our eyes!
We have finally captured the scourge of the known universe.
It will finally meet its fate after a thousand years of terror.
I am sending instructions to engage Tracker and fire the containment ship into Geon. That sun is becoming more unstable.
People of Earth and sister planets watch a fleet of TimeShips and the Containment Ship holding MicroV in deep space. The ships arrive at Geon, a massive black hole. It is sucking in matter from a sun crossing over in its event horizon.

DEEP WITHIN THE HULL OF THE CONTAINMENT SHIP
THE MicroV ENCASED IN CRYSTAL
AS THE FLEET OF TimeShips SOARS AWAY FROM THE BLACK HOLE, SUDDENLY, THE SUN EXPLODES, DESTROYING THE CONTAINMENT SHIP AND ALLOWING THE MicroV TO ESCAPE.
THE TRACKER FOLLOWS THE CRYSTAL AS IT SOARS INTO AN UNSTABLE DEEP SPACE CAUSED BY POWERFUL GRAVITATIONAL WAVES.
THE TRACKER ATTACHES TO THE MASSIVE CRYSTAL
M.O.M. MEMBERS WATCH IN HORROR.

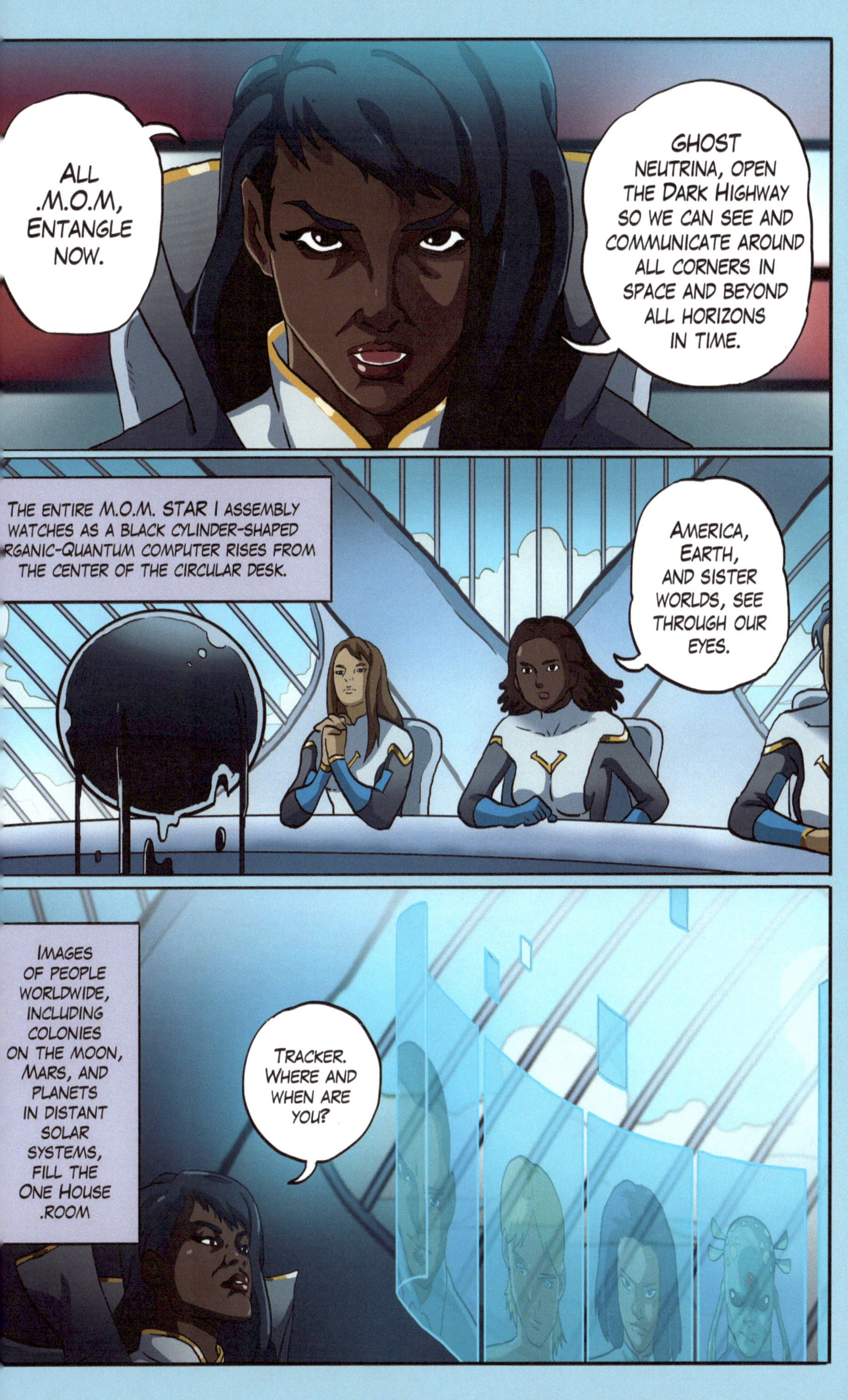

ALL .M.O.M, ENTANGLE NOW.
GHOST NEUTRINA, OPEN THE DARK HIGHWAY SO WE CAN SEE AND COMMUNICATE AROUND ALL CORNERS IN SPACE AND BEYOND ALL HORIZONS IN TIME.
THE ENTIRE M.O.M. STAR I ASSEMBLY WATCHES AS A BLACK CYLINDER-SHAPED ORGANIC-QUANTUM COMPUTER RISES FROM THE CENTER OF THE CIRCULAR DESK.
AMERICA, EARTH, AND SISTER WORLDS, SEE THROUGH OUR EYES.
IMAGES OF PEOPLE WORLDWIDE, INCLUDING COLONIES ON THE MOON, MARS, AND PLANETS IN DISTANT SOLAR SYSTEMS, FILL THE ONE HOUSE .ROOM
TRACKER. WHERE AND WHEN ARE YOU?

THE MASSIVE CRYSTAL SPEEDS PAST THE RINGS OF SATURN WITH TRACKER ATTACHED. THE COMPUTER DELIVERS THE UPDATE FROM TRACKER.
MicroV IS APPROACHING EARTH THIRTY THOUSAND YEARS IN YOUR PAST. THE CREATURE HAS MASTERED TIME TRAVEL. I WILL CONTINUE SENDING THE SPACETIME COORDINATES.
THE CRYSTAL APPROACHES EARTH AT SPEEDS BEYOND IMAGINATION.
THERE IS TIME TO SAVE THEM.
THE CREATURE WILL NEED TO HIBERNATE TO REGAIN ITS STRENGTH.
I HAVE EXHAUSTED MY SHIELD. I LOVE YOU ALL!
I WILL EXPIRE WHEN THE CRYSTAL ENTERS EARTH'S ATMOSPHERE.
30,000 YEARS IN THE FUTURE M.O.M. MEMBERS SPEAK TO TRACKER THROUGH TIME AND SPACE VIA THE POWER OF GHOST NEUTRINA.
TRACKER ENTERS HIGH EARTH ORBIT AS THE CRYSTAL CONTINUES TO THE EARTH BELOW.
I HAVE YOUR COORDINATES. I HAVE BAD NEWS FOR YOU. I HAVE A LOCK ON YOU. WE ARE LAUNCHING YOU INTO EARTH ORBIT FOR LATER RETRIEVAL.
SLEEP NOW. WHEN YOU AWAKE, YOU WILL HAVE MUCH MORE WORK TO DO.
HARRIET ADDRESSES THE ENTIRE GROUP.
PLEASANT DREAMS. WE LOVE YOU, TOO!
THE CREATURE HAS INVADED OUR HOME. IT ENDS NOW! THEY WILL NOT PERISH!

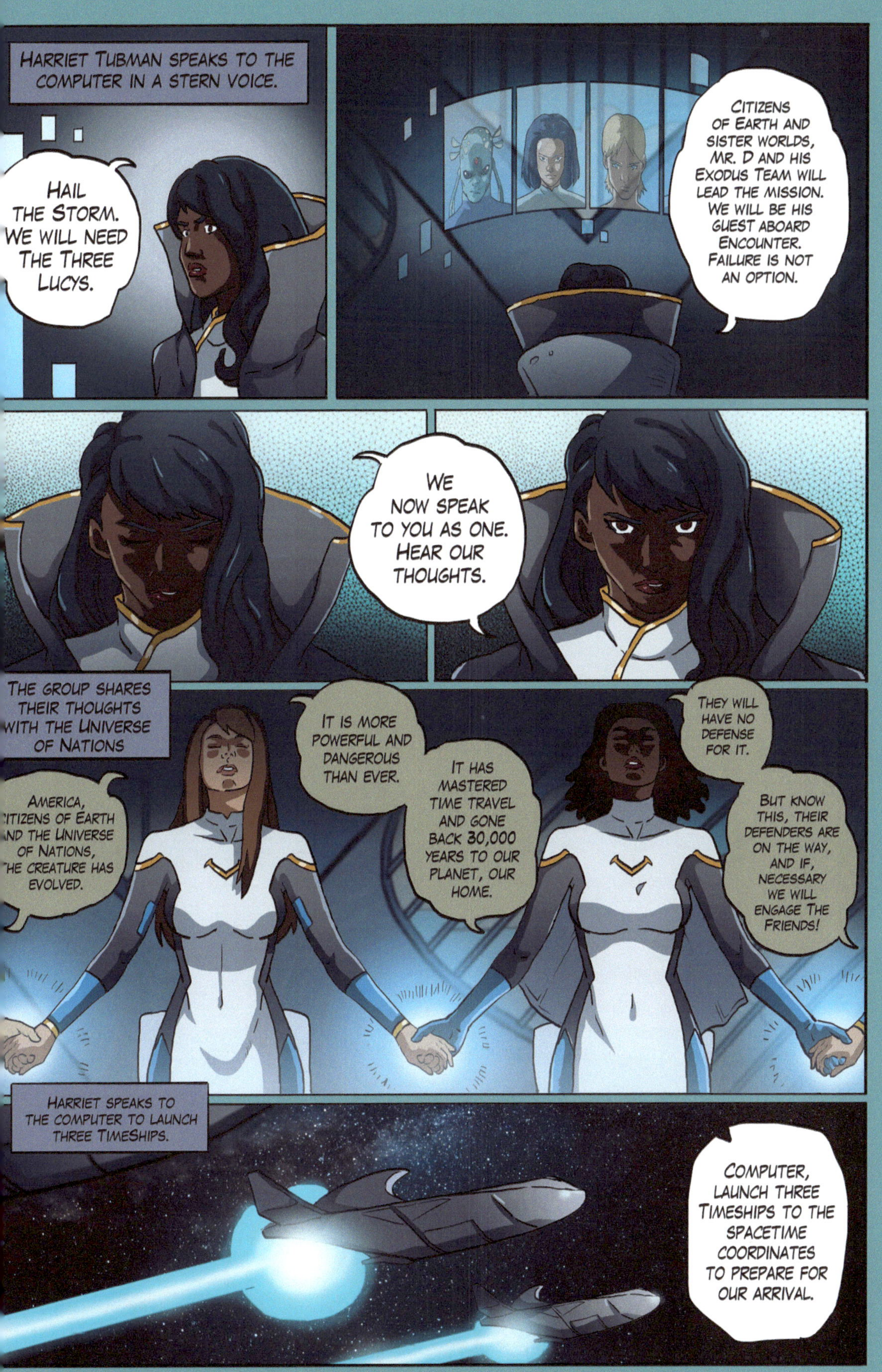

HARRIET TUBMAN SPEAKS TO THE COMPUTER IN A STERN VOICE.
HAIL THE STORM. WE WILL NEED THE THREE LUCYS.
CITIZENS OF EARTH AND SISTER WORLDS, MR. D AND HIS EXODUS TEAM WILL LEAD THE MISSION. WE WILL BE HIS GUEST ABOARD ENCOUNTER. FAILURE IS NOT AN OPTION.
WE NOW SPEAK TO YOU AS ONE. HEAR OUR THOUGHTS.
THE GROUP SHARES THEIR THOUGHTS WITH THE UNIVERSE OF NATIONS
AMERICA, CITIZENS OF EARTH AND THE UNIVERSE OF NATIONS, THE CREATURE HAS EVOLVED.
IT IS MORE POWERFUL AND DANGEROUS THAN EVER.
IT HAS MASTERED TIME TRAVEL AND GONE BACK 30,000 YEARS TO OUR PLANET, OUR HOME.
THEY WILL HAVE NO DEFENSE FOR IT.
BUT KNOW THIS, THEIR DEFENDERS ARE ON THE WAY, AND IF NECESSARY WE WILL ENGAGE THE FRIENDS!
HARRIET SPEAKS TO THE COMPUTER TO LAUNCH THREE TIMESHIPS.
COMPUTER, LAUNCH THREE TIMESHIPS TO THE SPACETIME COORDINATES TO PREPARE FOR OUR ARRIVAL.

THE PRESENT
THE 30-FOOT TALL CRYSTAL FLIES TOWARDS THE CASCADE CAVES IN THE MIXED MESOPHYTIC FORESTS OF EASTERN KENTUCKY.
IT HOVERS ABOVE THE LUSH VARIETIES OF FERNS, SMALL TREES, AND HERBACEOUS PLANTS.
THE CRYSTAL VIBRATES AND SLOWLY SINKS BENEATH THE GROUND.
LOWER
GONE
THE 30-FOOT TALL CRYSTAL EMERGES INTO A MASSIVE CAVE WITH WATER FLOWING THROUGH IT TO A TOWERING WATERFALL OUTSIDE.
DIM
DIMMER...
HIBERNATE

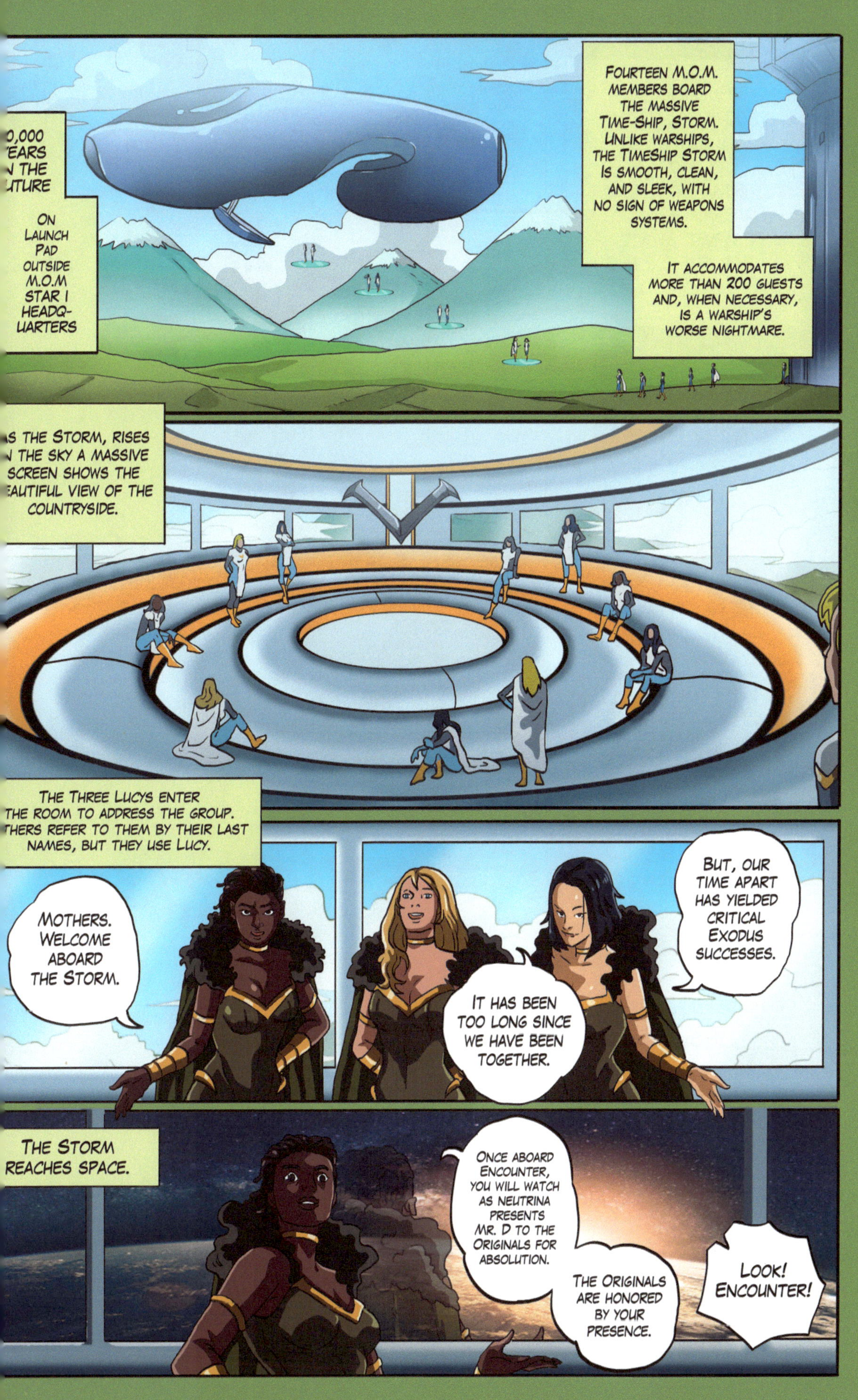

0,000 YEARS N THE UTURE

ON LAUNCH PAD OUTSIDE M.O.M STAR 1 HEADQUARTERS

FOURTEEN M.O.M. MEMBERS BOARD THE MASSIVE TIME-SHIP, STORM. UNLIKE WARSHIPS, THE TIMESHIP STORM IS SMOOTH, CLEAN, AND SLEEK, WITH NO SIGN OF WEAPONS SYSTEMS.

IT ACCOMMODATES MORE THAN 200 GUESTS AND, WHEN NECESSARY, IS A WARSHIP'S WORSE NIGHTMARE.

S THE STORM, RISES N THE SKY A MASSIVE SCREEN SHOWS THE EAUTIFUL VIEW OF THE COUNTRYSIDE.

THE THREE LUCYS ENTER THE ROOM TO ADDRESS THE GROUP. THERS REFER TO THEM BY THEIR LAST NAMES, BUT THEY USE LUCY.

MOTHERS. WELCOME ABOARD THE STORM.

IT HAS BEEN TOO LONG SINCE WE HAVE BEEN TOGETHER.

BUT, OUR TIME APART HAS YIELDED CRITICAL EXODUS SUCCESSES.

THE STORM REACHES SPACE.

ONCE ABOARD ENCOUNTER, YOU WILL WATCH AS NEUTRINA PRESENTS MR. D TO THE ORIGINALS FOR ABSOLUTION.

THE ORIGINALS ARE HONORED BY YOUR PRESENCE.

LOOK! ENCOUNTER!

ENCOUNTER- 500-KILOMETERS IN DIAMETER THE MOTHER-STAR-POWERED TIMESHIP EXPLICITLY DESIGNED BY MR. D FOR THE EXODUS PROJECT.
PERMANENT RESIDENCY, UNKNOWN. ONCE ABOARD, DESIGNATED AREAS REPLICATE THE PLANETARY ENVIRONMENTS OF THE GUESTS.
IT INCLUDES THEIR HOMES BY REQUEST, INCLUDING THE WILDLIFE, WEATHER, AND GRAVITY LEVELS.

HUNTING IS NOT ALLOWED. EACH CREW MEMBER IS BIO-TECHNICALLY MATCHED TO THEIR PERSONAL SKYCYCLE AND CAN TIME-TRAVEL POWERED BY ENCOUNTER.
SPORTS TEAMS RIVAL ANY ON EARTH.

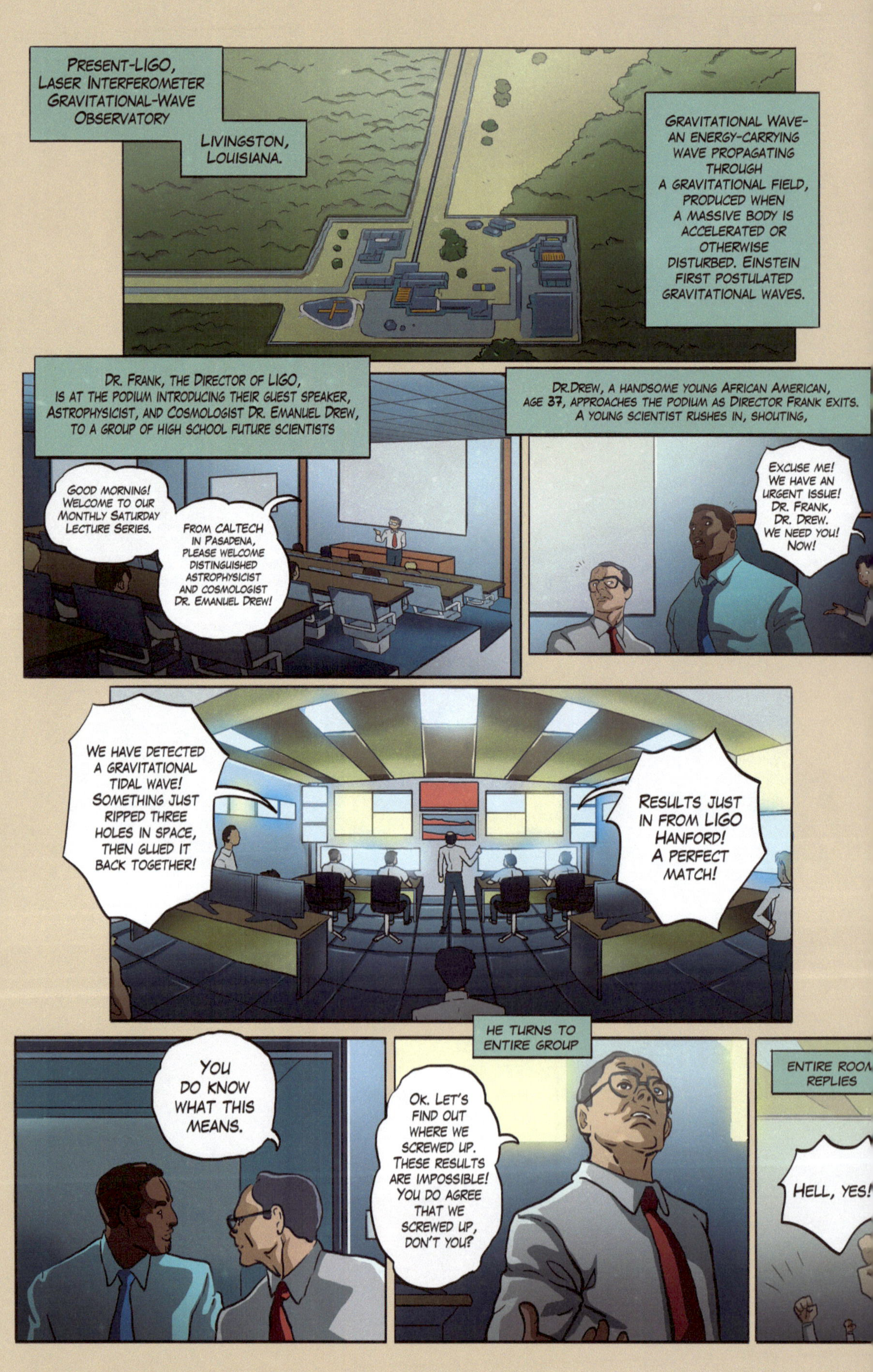

PRESENT-LIGO, LASER INTERFEROMETER GRAVITATIONAL-WAVE OBSERVATORY
LIVINGSTON, LOUISIANA.
GRAVITATIONAL WAVE- AN ENERGY-CARRYING WAVE PROPAGATING THROUGH A GRAVITATIONAL FIELD, PRODUCED WHEN A MASSIVE BODY IS ACCELERATED OR OTHERWISE DISTURBED. EINSTEIN FIRST POSTULATED GRAVITATIONAL WAVES.
DR. FRANK, THE DIRECTOR OF LIGO, IS AT THE PODIUM INTRODUCING THEIR GUEST SPEAKER, ASTROPHYSICIST, AND COSMOLOGIST DR. EMANUEL DREW, TO A GROUP OF HIGH SCHOOL FUTURE SCIENTISTS
GOOD MORNING! WELCOME TO OUR MONTHLY SATURDAY LECTURE SERIES.
FROM CALTECH IN PASADENA, PLEASE WELCOME DISTINGUISHED ASTROPHYSICIST AND COSMOLOGIST DR. EMANUEL DREW!
DR. DREW, A HANDSOME YOUNG AFRICAN AMERICAN, AGE 37, APPROACHES THE PODIUM AS DIRECTOR FRANK EXITS. A YOUNG SCIENTIST RUSHES IN, SHOUTING,
EXCUSE ME! WE HAVE AN URGENT ISSUE! DR. FRANK, DR. DREW. WE NEED YOU! NOW!
WE HAVE DETECTED A GRAVITATIONAL TIDAL WAVE! SOMETHING JUST RIPPED THREE HOLES IN SPACE, THEN GLUED IT BACK TOGETHER!
RESULTS JUST IN FROM LIGO HANFORD! A PERFECT MATCH!
YOU DO KNOW WHAT THIS MEANS.
HE TURNS TO ENTIRE GROUP
OK. LET'S FIND OUT WHERE WE SCREWED UP. THESE RESULTS ARE IMPOSSIBLE! YOU DO AGREE THAT WE SCREWED UP, DON'T YOU?
ENTIRE ROOM REPLIES
HELL, YES!

DIRECTOR FRANK ADDRESSES THE STAFF
RUN SILENT, FOLKS! NO LEAKS!
START SEARCHING! LOOK UNDER EVERY ASTEROID! FIND THE ERROR!
DIRECTOR FRANK SPEAKS TO DR. DREW QUIETLY WITH A LOOK OF GRAVE CONCERN.
WE WILL NEED YOUR EYES ON THIS ONE, MANNY.
TO QUOTE SHERLOCK HOLMES,
"WHEN YOU ELIMINATE ALL THAT IS, IMPOSSIBLE WHATEVER REMAINS MUST BE THE TRUTH, NO MATTER HOW IMPROBABLE"
YOU HAD THE SAME CONCERNS WHEN YOU PROVED THE EXISTENCE OF GRAVITATIONAL WAVES, FOR WHICH YOU WON THE NOBEL PRIZE. I SERIOUSLY DOUBT YOUR TEAM MISSED ANYTHING. THEY TRAINED UNDER YOU.
THE ENERGY REQUIRED TO CREATE A GRAVITATIONAL DISTURBANCE OF THIS MAGNITUDE, WELL, WHATEVER IT IS, YOU HAVE DISCOVERED AN EVENT BEYOND COMPREHENSION! HOPEFULLY, IT HAPPENED MILLIONS OR BILLIONS OF YEARS AGO IN A DISTANT GALAXY.
BUT THAT MAKES NO SENSE.
LOOK, I HAVE A LECTURE TO GIVE, ASSUMING THEY ARE STILL THERE. PLEASE SEND THE COORDINATES ASAP. OH, I HAVE MORE BAD NEWS
FOR YOU. I HEAR YOUR GRANDSON'S TEAM PLANS TO TRAVEL TO L.A. FOR THE A.A.U. BASKETBALL TOURNAMENT THIS SUMMER.
WHY IS THAT BAD NEWS?
HE'S IN THE SAME AGE GROUP AS MY BOY.
DAMN! YOU DO KNOW I'M COMING WITH THEM!
DINNER ON ME! IT IS THE LEAST I CAN DO!

THE DISTURBANCE ORIGINATED WITHIN THE ASTEROID BELT NEAR. CERES
DWARF PLANET CERES - THE LARGEST OBJECT IN THE ASTEROID BELT BETWEEN MARS AND THE LARGEST PLANET IN THE SOLAR SYSTEM, JUPITER.

WHILE STUDYING THE REPORT, DR. FRANK SPEAKS TO THE SCIENTIST AS DR. LEE WATCHES.
I OWE YOU ONE. TELL DR. DREW WE WILL BE MEETING IN HEAD SCRATCHER.
YOU PLAYED BASEBALL IN COLLEGE, DIDN'T YOU? EVER PINCH HIT?
I'LL TAKE OVER FOR DR. DREW. I WILL GIVE THEM MY FAMOUS "DARK MATTER" LECTURE.
THE DISTURBANCE IS HAPPENING IN REAL-TIME IN OUR BACKYARD. WHATEVER CAUSED IT IS NOT FROM HERE, AND I'M AFRAID TO FIND OUT WHAT IT IS.
WHAT ABOUT THE PARKER SOLAR PROBE OR JAMES WEBB? WE COULD REDIRECT THEM TO LOOK TOWARD CERES.
LET'S TURN EVERY EYE IN THE SKY TOWARDS CERES.
WE ALSO NEED TO WAKE UP DAWN AND HAVE HER TAKE A LOOK AROUND.

MANNY, SHE DIED!
NASA HAS LOTS OF MAD. SCIENTISTS I'M SURE AT LEAST ONE OF THEM IS NAMED VICTOR. WE WILL NEED DETAILED IMAGES OF CERES; ALSO PHOTOS LOOKING OUT FROM CERES TOWARDS SPACE, IF POSSIBLE.
FRANK. CAN I TALK WITH YOU AND JANE BEFORE I TAKE OFF? JOYCE GETS ANGRY IF I AM GONE FOR MORE THAN TWENTY. YEARS
LIGO HALLWAY OUTSIDE THE HEAD SCRATCHER CONFERENCE ROOM.
I'M SURE YOU REALIZE THIS NOW HAS POTENTIAL NATIONAL SECURITY IMPLICATIONS. WE SHOULD ENGAGE THE APPROPRIATE AGENCIES IMMEDIATELY.
AGREE
I AGREE.

DR. DREW PAUSES AS HE WALKS AWAY
OH! WHEN I RETURNED TO THE LECTURE, THE STUDENTS HAD RESOLVED DARK MATTER, SLOWED THE EXPANDING UNIVERSE AND UNTIED, THE KNOTS IN STRING THEORY. HIRE THEM ALL!

PRESENT
SPACE SOLAR SYSTEM
THE DWARF PLANET CERES
GIANT FLOATING TANKER SPACESHIP SUCKS TONS OF DIRTY WATER ICE FROM THE BASE OF A WALL INSIDE A CRATER ON CERES AS ANOTHER FULL OF ICE LEAVES FOR ONE OF THE THREE ADVANCE SHIPS DEPLOYED BY M.O.M.
THE TANKERS DELIVER THE WATER ICE TO ONE OF M.O.M'S VASTLY LARGER TIMESHIPS SENT FROM THE FUTURE.

PRESENT
SANTA MONICA
LINCOLN MIDDLE SCHOOL
KHALID, AGE 10, DR. DREW'S SON, A 6TH-GRADER, IS ALONE AT HIS HALLWAY LOCKER.
HE DOESN'T SEE THREE BOYS APPROACHING FROM BEHIND.
THE BIGGEST KID, TODD, BANGS THE LOCKER NEXT TO KHALID.
BANG!
KHALID DOESN'T REACT TO THE LOUD BANG.
KHALID SPEAKS WITHOUT LOOKING TO SEE WHO IS BEHIND HIM.
LUNCH ON THE BACKCOURT.
YEAH.
NOTHING RADDLES HIM.
NOTHING.

SAME DAY, SANTA MONICA, LINCOLN MIDDLE SCHOOL LUNCH BREAK, BACK BASKETBALL COURTS.
HERE COMES THAT KID YOU TRIED TO SCARE. YOU SAID YOU WOULD TEACH US HANDLES TO HELP US MAKE THE TEAM.
KHALID, YEAH!
HE'S MY BEST FRIEND. WE WERE JUST MESSIN' WITH YOU GUYS. HE'S THE BEST BALLER I'VE EVER SEEN. YOU SAID YOU WANTED HANDLES. HE'S THE MAN.
THE SAME THREE STUDENTS ARE ON THE COURT. ONE TAKES SHOTS. THE OTHER BOY TALKS TO TODD AS KHALID APPROACHES WITH HIS BASKETBALL
KHALID PERFORMS SERIES OF QUICK DRILLS.
LET'S DO THIS! WATCH!
THEY WATCH IN AMAZEMENT AS KHALID PERFORMS BALL-HANDLING DRILLS.
HANDLES ARE IMPORTANT, BUT TEAM PLAY WINS GAMES, AND DEFENSE WINS CHAMPIONSHIPS. WE START TODAY. I WILL TEXT YOUR READING ASSIGNMENT. STUDY AND RESPECT THE GAME TO LOVE THE GAME.
LIKE YOU SAID, LET'S DO THIS!
RIGHT HERE, SAME TIME EVERY DAY.
KHALID PAUSES AND LOOKS SKYWARD.
WHAT?
THEY'RE WATCHING US.
WHO? SECURITY CAMERAS?
NO.
FROM SPACE.

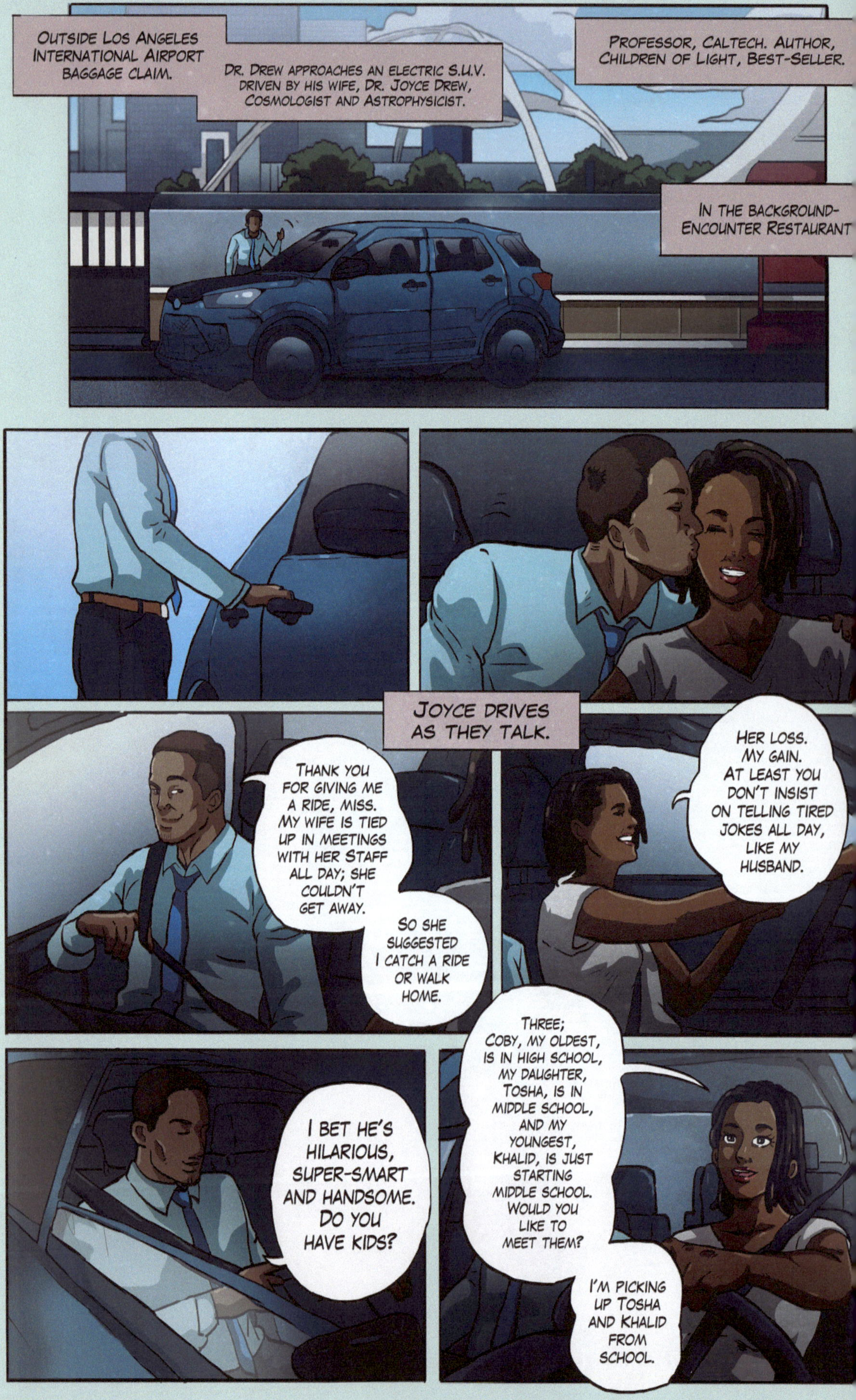

OUTSIDE LOS ANGELES INTERNATIONAL AIRPORT BAGGAGE CLAIM.
DR. DREW APPROACHES AN ELECTRIC S.U.V. DRIVEN BY HIS WIFE, DR. JOYCE DREW, COSMOLOGIST AND ASTROPHYSICIST.
PROFESSOR, CALTECH. AUTHOR, CHILDREN OF LIGHT, BEST-SELLER.
IN THE BACKGROUND-ENCOUNTER RESTAURANT
JOYCE DRIVES AS THEY TALK.
THANK YOU FOR GIVING ME A RIDE, MISS. MY WIFE IS TIED UP IN MEETINGS WITH HER STAFF ALL DAY; SHE COULDN'T GET AWAY.
SO SHE SUGGESTED I CATCH A RIDE OR WALK HOME.
HER LOSS. MY GAIN. AT LEAST YOU DON'T INSIST ON TELLING TIRED JOKES ALL DAY, LIKE MY HUSBAND.
I BET HE'S HILARIOUS, SUPER-SMART AND HANDSOME. DO YOU HAVE KIDS?
THREE; COBY, MY OLDEST, IS IN HIGH SCHOOL, MY DAUGHTER, TOSHA, IS IN MIDDLE SCHOOL, AND MY YOUNGEST, KHALID, IS JUST STARTING MIDDLE SCHOOL. WOULD YOU LIKE TO MEET THEM?
I'M PICKING UP TOSHA AND KHALID FROM SCHOOL.

I'D LOVE TO MEET YOUR KIDS. BUT KNOW THIS: I'M NOT GOOD WITH KIDS.
THEY TALK FUNNY AND DON'T UNDERSTAND GRAVITY.
THEY DROP THINGS,
PUT THINGS DOWN, AND KNOCK THINGS OVER.
AND?
AFTER MONTHS OF DOING THIS, THEY SEEM SHOCKED THAT THE STUFF IS STILL THERE.
YOU SOUND A LOT LIKE MY HUSBAND. I'M HAVING SECOND THOUGHTS ABOUT YOU MEETING MY KIDS.
PLEASE! I'LL BE NICE.
OK, BUT I'LL BE WATCHING YOU!
WOW! YOU TWO HAVE REALLY GROWN! I HARDLY RECOGNIZED YOU!
I MISSED YOU SO MUCH! IT'S BEEN SO LONG!
FIVE DAYS, DAD!

FIVE DAYS! YOU SURE?
FIVE DAYS WITH NO JOKES. COOL! BUT WE DID MISS YOU.

HONEY! NO JOKES! I LEFT YOU A LIST!
IT'S A LONG WALK .HOME

INSIDE THE S.U.V.
KIDS! YOU MUST PRETEND TO BE HAPPY TO SEE YOUR MOM. REMEMBER, SHE LIVES WITH US, TOO.

OK, IF YOU INSIST!

ENOUGH ALREADY! COBY'S WAITING FOR US!

I'LL GET HIM.

BEFORE
E STARTS
ITH THE
XCUSES,
I WON.
AND HYENAS LOVE LIONS.
HI DAD!
O EASY
N HIM.
S FRAGILE,
T THERE'S
E. PLEASE
IVE MY
EGARDS
O YOUR
ARENTS.
I WILL, AND MY DAD SAID TO TELL YOU THAT WAS A LUCKY PUTT, WHATEVER THAT MEANS.
EVERYONE! COBY WAS DOING SHOOTING DRILLS WITH MIA. SADLY, HE HAD TO WAIT UNTIL AFTER SCHOOL TO GET SCHOOLED.
IT WAS. BUT DON'T TELL HIM I ADMITTED IT.
DON'T YOU AVE ANOTHER EMERGENCY RIP TO TAKE?
UNFORTUNATELY, I DO.

LATER - DRIVING HOME ON A QUIET NEIGHBORHOOD STREET - KHALID SCREAMS AS THEY APPROACH THE INTERSECTION WITH A GREEN LIGHT!
MOM!
STOP!
JOYCE BARELY AVOIDS HITTING A CAR RUNNING THE RED LIGHT.
EVERYONE IS AMAZED THAT KHALID KNEW A CAR HE COULDN'T SEE WOULD RUN THE LIGHT.
YOU WHAT!
I COULD HEAR HER ON THE PHONE DISTRACTED DRIVING.
MOM! DAD!
CHECK HIS ROOM FOR SPIDERS!

LATER
IN THEIR DRIVEWAY. JOYCE AND MANNY STAY IN THE CAR AS THE KIDS ENTER THE HOUSE.
I KNOW YOU ARE WONDERING THE SAME THING AS ME.
HOW DID HE KNOW IT WAS A WOMAN DRIVER?
THAT SHE... WAS ON HER PHONE AND WOULD RUN THE LIGHT?
DO YOU THINK HE MIGHT BE A SUPERHERO?
WELL, HE'S CERTAINLY MY HERO, BUT JUST IN CASE, CHECK HIS ROOM FOR SPIDERS.
HE MAY HAVE JUST SAVED OUR LIVES.
KHALID RELAXES ON HIS BED, READING A BOOK. THE TITLE - "DOUGLASS."

30,00 YEARS IN THE FUTURE

M.O.M. MEMBERS WATCH A HUGE SCREEN IN A CHAMBER ABOARD ENCOUNTER. MR. D, TAU, TRONA, AND MU NEUTRINA STAND WITH A DELEGATION OF NATIVE AMERICANS AND POWERFUL 8-FOOT-TALL ALIENS IN THE CENTER OF A PACKED, FUTURISTIC OUTDOOR STADIUM.

YOU HAVE STOOD BESIDE MR. D AS HE SERVED HIS PENANCE.

TAU NEUTRINA STEPS FORWARD AS A FEMALE NATIVE AMERICAN SPEAKS HER NATIVE TONGUE.

WE EMBRACE HIM FOR HIS DEEDS, HIS WISDOM, AND HUMILITY. NOW, WE ARE ONE.

RETRACT YOUR FACE SHIELD. NOW, YOU ARE ONE WITH US FOREVER,

IT IS TIME!

A FRIEND, A BROTHER, A CHAMPION.

A GIFT FOR MR. D FROM THE THOUSANDS OF WORLDS AND BILLIONS OF LIVES
HE HAS SAVED. ITS POWERS ARE BEYOND BELIEF.
TAU NEUTRINA IS PRESENTED WITH A FOLDED BLACK CAPE FOR MR. D BY THE 8-FOOT TALL ALIEN. MR. D, HIS FACE SHIELDED, NOW LIES IN A BLACK DISC IN A MOLD SHAPED TO FIT HIS BODY EXACTLY.
THEY SLOWLY RISE INTO THE SKY WITH THE DISC..
ONCE ABOVE THE STADIUM, THEY STOP.
ABOARD ENCOUNTER
WE ARE READY.
PREPARE HIM, THEN FLY HIM INTO THE MOUTH OF THE DRAGN. HE IS THE MOST POWERFUL NOW.
SOON, HE WILL BE REBORN- INVINCIBLE.

THE TIME-SHIP SHADOW ARRIVES FAR INTO DEEP SPACE NEAR A POWERFUL QUASAR SHINING A BILLION TIMES BRIGHTER THAN THE SUN CREATED BY A SUPERMASSIVE BLACK HOLE CONSUMING LARGE AMOUNTS OF MATTER. IT EMITS POLAR JETS OF RADIATION, SHOOTING MILLIONS OF LIGHT-YEARS INTO SPACE SCIENTISTS CALL A DRAGN.
SHADOW LAUNCHES THE DISC CONTAINING MR. D INTO THE HOT TIP OF THE DRAGN.

AN INVINCIBLE MR. D IS BORN!

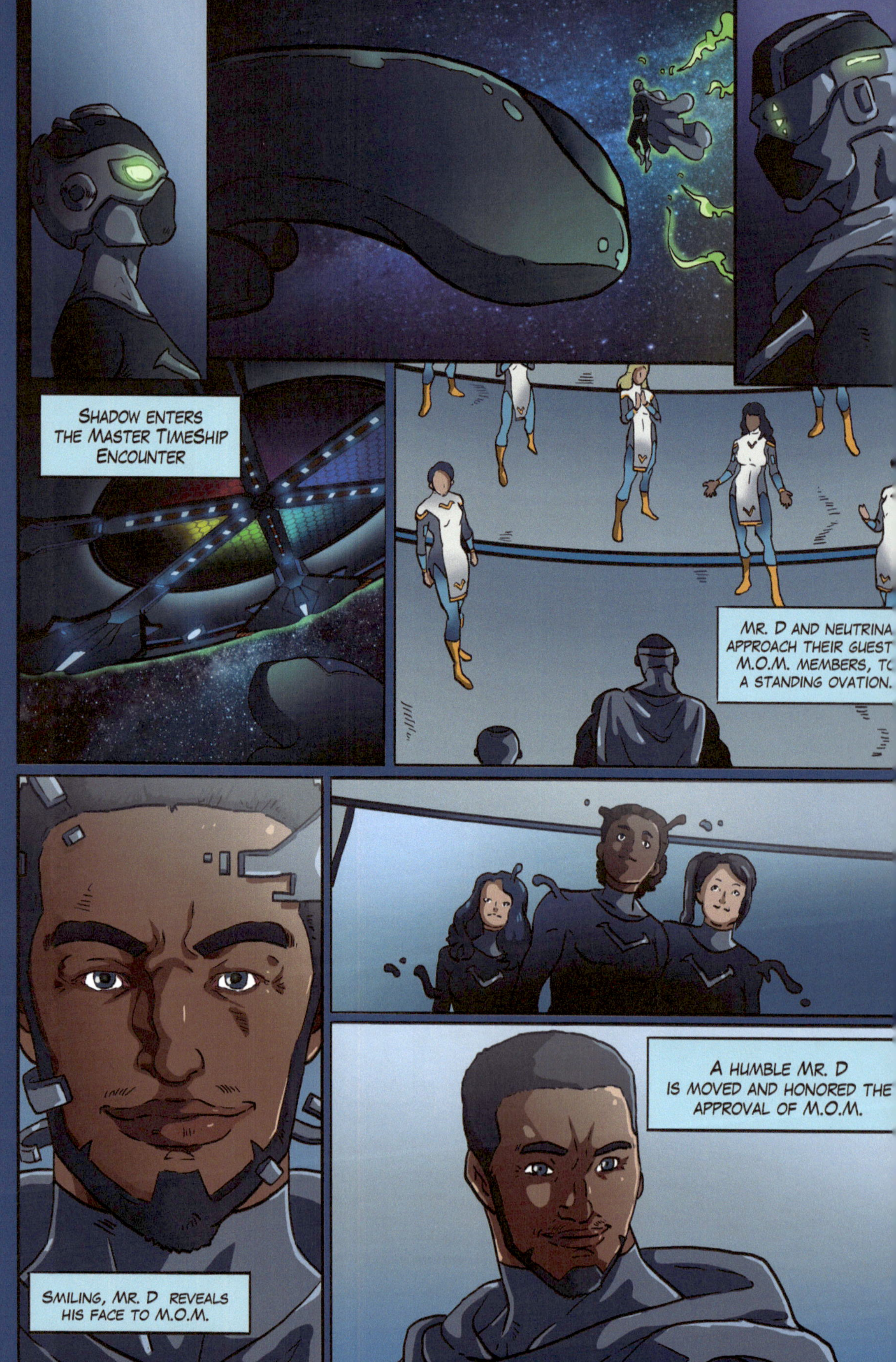

SHADOW ENTERS THE MASTER TIMESHIP ENCOUNTER
MR. D AND NEUTRINA APPROACH THEIR GUEST M.O.M. MEMBERS, TO A STANDING OVATION.
SMILING, MR. D REVEALS HIS FACE TO M.O.M.
A HUMBLE MR. D IS MOVED AND HONORED THE APPROVAL OF M.O.M.

WE ARE HUMBLED AND HONORED BY YOUR PRESENCE.
WE, TOO, ARE HONORED. BILLIONS ARE ALIVE
AND FREE BECAUSE OF YOU. NOW THAT YOU POSSESS THE POWER OF THE DRAGN, YOU WILL BRING HOPE BEYOND THE MILKY WAY, BEYOND OUR UNIVERSE.
WE MUST TURN TO THE MATTER THAT BRINGS US HERE. THE CREATURE HAS MASTERED TIME TRAVEL. EARTH IS IN PERIL. WE MUST GO. WILL YOU TAKE THE LEAD?
I WILL.
HE PAUSES AND LOOKS TOWARD WOMEN IN THE GROUP, SUSAN LA ESCHE AND SARAH WINNEMUCCA.
WITH YOUR PERMISSION.
THE ORIGINALS NATIONS OF ALL PLANETS ARE WITH YOU.
I AM GRATEFUL.

THIS IS YOUR MOMENT
TRAVEL BACK AND LEAD THE ADVANCE TEAM AS THEY PREPARE EARTH FOR OUR ARRIVAL.
NEUTRINA RISES HIGHER AND HIGHER.
SHE DISAPPEARS.

PRESENT DAY
HIGH EARTH ORBIT
NEUTRINA FLOATS WITH A FANTASTIC VIEW OF EARTH BELOW
TRACKER. WAKE UP. IT'S TIME FOR BREAKFAST.
NEUTRINA FLIES OFF TO MEET THE THREE ADVAMCE SHIP.
NEUTRINA SUDDENLY STOPS, LOOKS DOWN AT EARTH, AND UTTERS ONE WORD.
SPIDERS.
SHE FLIES OFF. INTO SPACE AT AN EXTREME SPEED

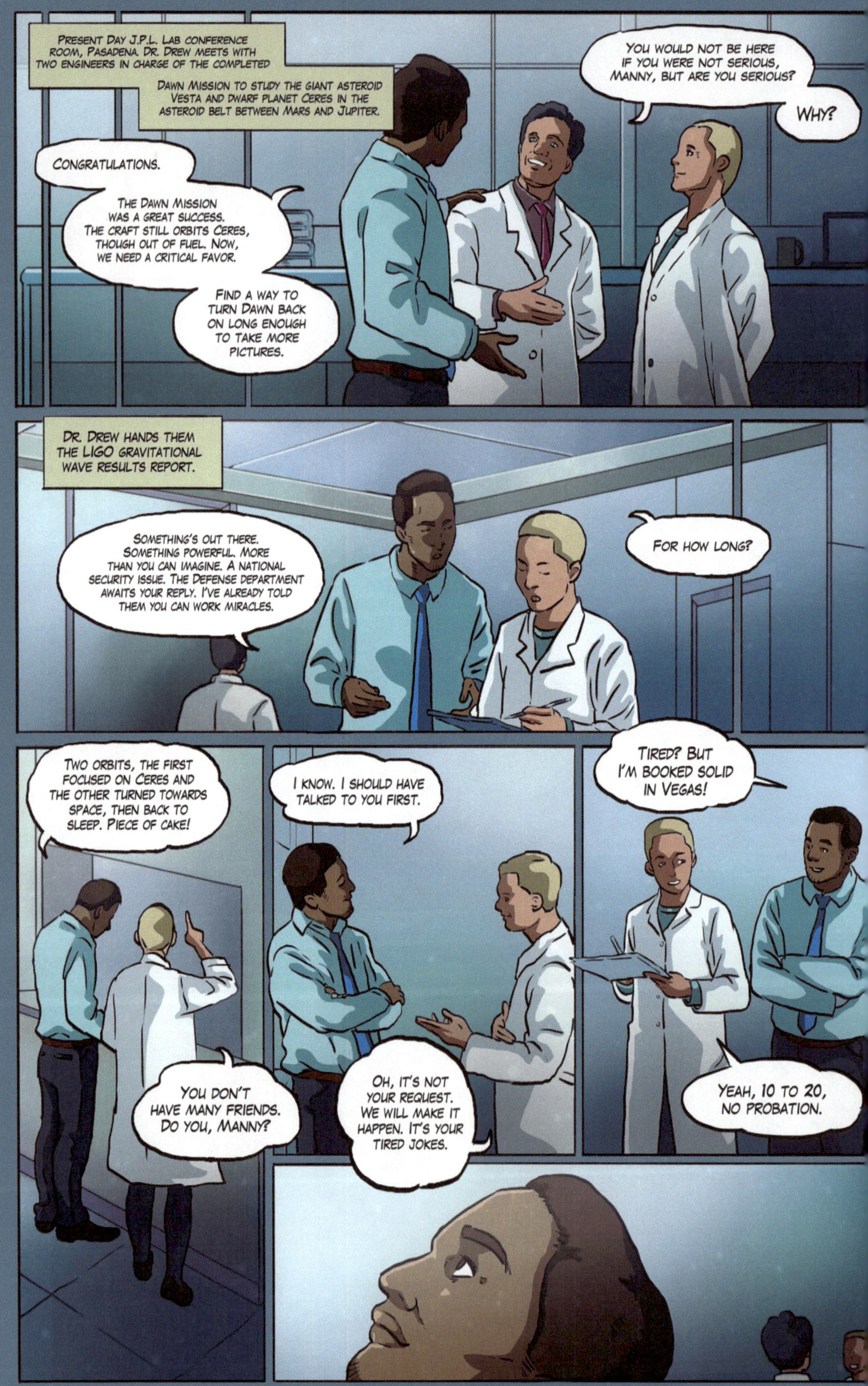
PRESENT DAY J.P.L. LAB CONFERENCE ROOM, PASADENA. DR. DREW MEETS WITH TWO ENGINEERS IN CHARGE OF THE COMPLETED
DAWN MISSION TO STUDY THE GIANT ASTEROID VESTA AND DWARF PLANET CERES IN THE ASTEROID BELT BETWEEN MARS AND JUPITER.
YOU WOULD NOT BE HERE IF YOU WERE NOT SERIOUS, MANNY, BUT ARE YOU SERIOUS?
WHY?
CONGRATULATIONS.
THE DAWN MISSION WAS A GREAT SUCCESS. THE CRAFT STILL ORBITS CERES, THOUGH OUT OF FUEL. NOW, WE NEED A CRITICAL FAVOR.
FIND A WAY TO TURN DAWN BACK ON LONG ENOUGH TO TAKE MORE PICTURES.
DR. DREW HANDS THEM THE LIGO GRAVITATIONAL WAVE RESULTS REPORT.
SOMETHING'S OUT THERE. SOMETHING POWERFUL. MORE THAN YOU CAN IMAGINE. A NATIONAL SECURITY ISSUE. THE DEFENSE DEPARTMENT AWAITS YOUR REPLY. I'VE ALREADY TOLD THEM YOU CAN WORK MIRACLES.
FOR HOW LONG?
TWO ORBITS, THE FIRST FOCUSED ON CERES AND THE OTHER TURNED TOWARDS SPACE, THEN BACK TO SLEEP. PIECE OF CAKE!
I KNOW. I SHOULD HAVE TALKED TO YOU FIRST.
TIRED? BUT I'M BOOKED SOLID IN VEGAS!
YOU DON'T HAVE MANY FRIENDS. DO YOU, MANNY?
OH, IT'S NOT YOUR REQUEST. WE WILL MAKE IT HAPPEN. IT'S YOUR TIRED JOKES.
YEAH, 10 TO 20, NO PROBATION.

PRESENT - ASTEROID BELT
THE DAWN CRAFT COMES ONLINE, READJUSTS ITS CAMERAS, AND BEGINS FILMING ITS TWO-ORBIT MISSION OF THE CERES DWARF PLANET.
MR. SECRETARY, WE CAN CONFIRM SOMETHING WAS OUT THERE AT CERES NEAR THE ORIGIN OF THE GRAVITATIONAL WAVES.
PRESENT DAY - WASHINGTON D.C.
A DEFENSE DEPARTMENT CONFERENCE ROOM THE SECRETARY OF DEFENSE, RETIRED FOUR-STAR AIR FORCE GENERAL JOSEPH DRAPER, AND THREE MILITARY MEMBERS ARE ON A VIDEO CONFERENCE WITH J.P.L. AND LIGO.
OUR SCAN SHOWS IT WAS THERE INTELLIGENCE-DRIVEN, AND FAR AHEAD OF OUR SPACE CAPABILITIES.
EXPLAIN, PLEASE.
DR. DREW DISPLAYS A PHOTO OF A LARGE CRATER ON CERES. IT SHOWS MASSIVE GAUGES CUT INTO THE SURFACE. HE POINTS TO THE CAVITIES WITHIN THE CRATERS.
TWENTY. WE WERE ABLE TO MAKE TWENTY ORBITS BEFORE SHUTTING DAWN DOWN AGAIN.
THESE OUTSTANDING ENGINEERS AWAKENED THE DAWN SPACECRAFT AND MADE TWO ORBITS OF CERES, CAPTURING THESE IMAGES THAT WILL REDEFINE EVERYTHING WE KNOW ABOUT OUR PLACE IN THE UNIVERSE.
WE ESTIMATE SOMETHING RECENTLY REMOVED ENOUGH WATER ICE FROM THE THREE CRATERS TO PROVIDE WATER TO NEW YORK CITY FOR FIVE YEARS.
I DO NOT HAVE TO SAY IT, DO I?
THE QUESTION IS WHO AND HOW? NO TECHNOLOGY EXISTS ON EARTH TO DO IT, AND FOR WHAT PURPOSE? AND WHAT SIZE VESSEL COULD HOLD THAT MUCH SURFACE MATERIAL? AND WHERE IS IT FROM, AND WHERE DID IT GO?
WE KNOW, SIR TOP SECRET.

Dr. Frank. Please express my gratitude to the LIGO teams at Livingston, Hanford, M.I.T. and Caltech.
You have put us on alert and possibly bought us much-needed time.

All of you, keep your bags packed. I'm on my way to the White House.
Dr. Drew, thank you for no bad jokes. I hear everything.

Mr. Secretary. There were three separate waves.
I would rather this be a joke, but there may be three vessels. We are ready when called.

Twenty orbits! Twenty orbits! You should all do Vegas! Vegas loves magic! You are the best! Now, I have an even more depressing meeting to attend.
Lives will be destroyed at NASA.

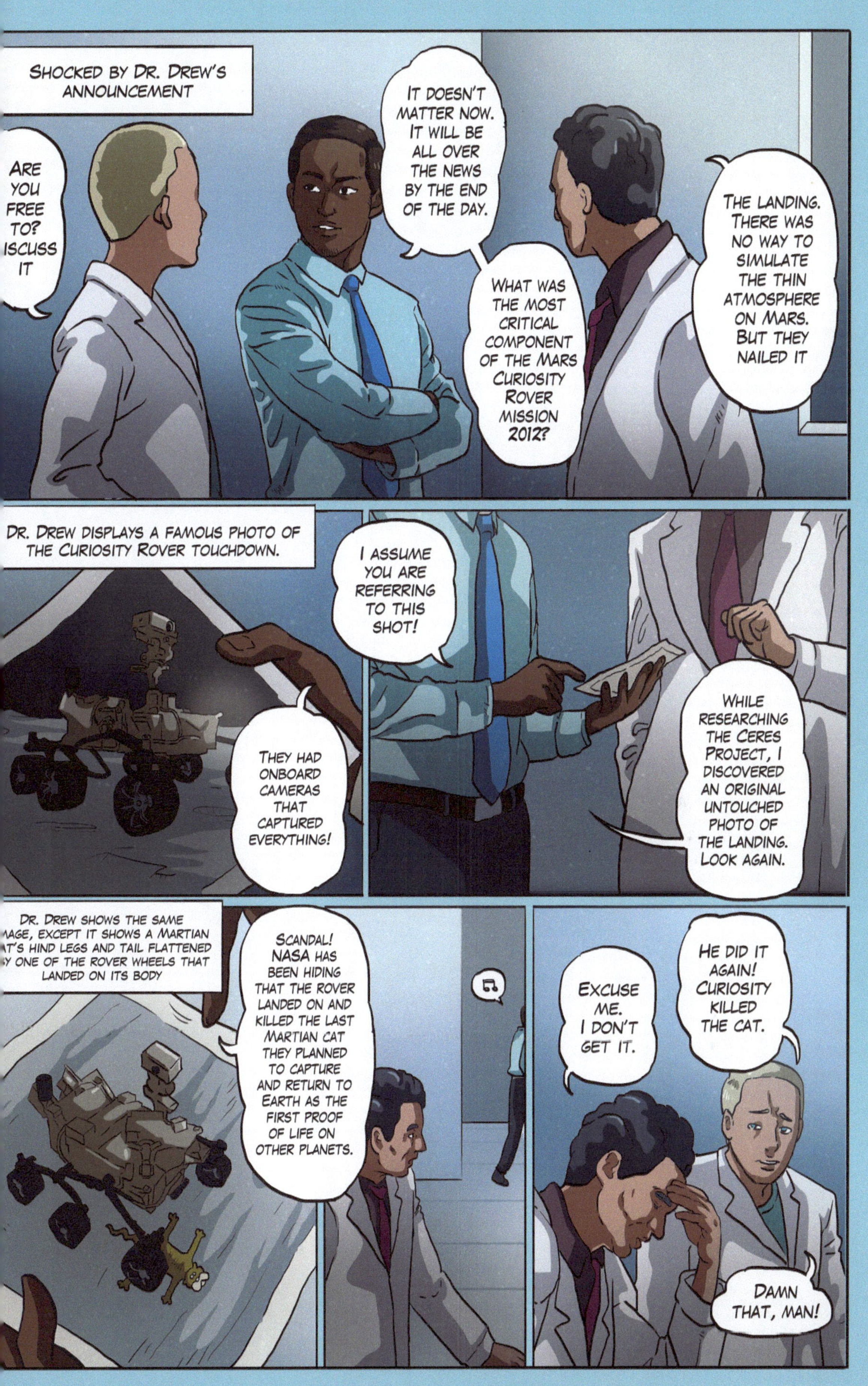

SHOCKED BY DR. DREW'S ANNOUNCEMENT
ARE YOU FREE TO? ISCUSS IT
IT DOESN'T MATTER NOW. IT WILL BE ALL OVER THE NEWS BY THE END OF THE DAY.
WHAT WAS THE MOST CRITICAL COMPONENT OF THE MARS CURIOSITY ROVER MISSION 2012?
THE LANDING. THERE WAS NO WAY TO SIMULATE THE THIN ATMOSPHERE ON MARS. BUT THEY NAILED IT
DR. DREW DISPLAYS A FAMOUS PHOTO OF THE CURIOSITY ROVER TOUCHDOWN.
I ASSUME YOU ARE REFERRING TO THIS SHOT!
THEY HAD ONBOARD CAMERAS THAT CAPTURED EVERYTHING!
WHILE RESEARCHING THE CERES PROJECT, I DISCOVERED AN ORIGINAL UNTOUCHED PHOTO OF THE LANDING. LOOK AGAIN.
DR. DREW SHOWS THE SAME IMAGE, EXCEPT IT SHOWS A MARTIAN CAT'S HIND LEGS AND TAIL FLATTENED BY ONE OF THE ROVER WHEELS THAT LANDED ON ITS BODY
SCANDAL! NASA HAS BEEN HIDING THAT THE ROVER LANDED ON AND KILLED THE LAST MARTIAN CAT THEY PLANNED TO CAPTURE AND RETURN TO EARTH AS THE FIRST PROOF OF LIFE ON OTHER PLANETS.
EXCUSE ME. I DON'T GET IT.
HE DID IT AGAIN! CURIOSITY KILLED THE CAT.
DAMN THAT, MAN!

ONE NEUTRINA ENTERS EACH ADVANCE TIME-SHIP.
INSIDE ONE TIMESHIP, TRONA NEUTRINA, NO LONGER WEARING HER HEADSHIELD, STANDS ALONE IN A MASSIVE EMPTY ROOM
WITH BOTH ARMS RAISED AS IF SHE IS WAITING FOR SOMETHING TO COME TO .HER FROM ABOVE
HUNDREDS OF THOUSANDS OF BASEBALL-SIZED DARK BALLS FLY DOWN FROM ABOVE AND SWARM AROUND HER LIKE BATS.

EACH NEUTRINA RISES FROM THE FLOOR AND EMITS A POWERFUL GLOW OF PURE ENERGY THAT TRANSFERS TO EACH BALL.
HUNDREDS OF THOUSANDS OF RECON BALLS FLY OUT OF THE EXHAUSTS ATOP THE ADVANCE TIME-SHIPS TOWARDS A DISTANT EARTH.
TRACKER.
YOU ARE EVERYWHERE NOW
FOR. M.O.M

THE PRESENT, EARTH. LATE NIGHT
J.F.K. TO L.A.X. RED-EYE FLIGHT, 30,000 FEET. MOST PASSENGERS ARE SLEEPING. THE LIGHTS DIMMED.
THE COCKPIT CREW CLOSELY MONITORS THE SCREEN SHOWING THE RADAR OF THE STORMS AHEAD.
THIS IS YOUR ILOT SPEAKING. WE WILL TAKE A SLIGHT DETOUR TO AVOID WEATHER AND CHOPPY AIR AHEAD. PLEASE RETURN TO YOUR SEATS AND FASTEN YOUR SEATBELTS.
AIR WEST 517 CLEAR TO TURN RIGHT TO HEADING 360.
CENTER, AIR WEST 517, REQUESTING A HEADING OF 360 FOR 50 MILES TO AVOID WEATHER.
AIR WEST 517 TURNING RIGHT TO HEADING 360.

As the plane banks, they are shocked to see they are flying directly into an enormous black structure rising out of the clouds below into space.

What the hell!

No!

Mayday!

Mayday!

Mayday!

Massive object in the flight path! Taking evasive maneuvers!

Please repeat! There is nothing on our radar in your flight path!

A SHORT TIME LATER...
MAYDAY, MAYDAY, MAYDAY REQUEST EMERGENCY LANDING AT ST. LOUIS INTERNATIONAL!
LATE NIGHT - ST. LOUIS INTERNATIONAL AIRPORT REMOTE RUNWAY AREA EMERGENCY VEHICLES ASSIST PASSENGERS OFF THE PLANE AND BOARDING BUSES.
THE PILOTS AND CREW ARE LOADED INTO A VAN, ESCORTED BY AIRPORT SECURITY AND FAA OFFICIALS.

BOARDING THE VAN TO CARRY THE CREW ACROSS THE TARMAC TO THE TERMINAL
YOU HAVE THE COORDINATES. DO WE HAVE PLANES IN THE SKY?
WHAT, EXACTLY, DID YOU SEE?
A HOLE THE SIZE OF NEW YORK IN THE SKY. WE ALMOST FLEW DIRECTLY INTO IT.
I LOOKED OUT A WINDOW. THE SKY WAS GONE.

THE CO-PILOT INTERRUPTS.
A DAMN HOLE IN THE SKY!
WERE THERE ANY INJURIES AMONG THE PASSENGERS?
NONE. THANKS TO YOU AND YOUR ENTIRE CREW.

THANK YOU. WE NEED TO TALK TO THE PASSENGERS. WE OWE THEM AN EXPLANATION.
OK, BUT PLEASE LIMIT HOW MUCH INFORMATION YOU SHARE. ALL FLIGHTS NEAR THE COORDINATES YOU SENT ARE GROUNDED.
ONLY RECON FLIGHTS ARE IN THE SKY. SO FAR, NOTHING TO REPORT.
LATE NIGHT
HOME OF JOYCE AND MANNY DREW.
THE KIDS ARE IN BED. JOYCE AND MANNY ARE SITTING ON THE FLOOR IN THEIR DEN, WORKING TOGETHER ON THEIR LAPTOPS. JOYCE IS READING MANNY'S REPORT ON GRAVITATIONAL WAVES.
IF THESE PICTURES OF CERES ARE ACCURATE, SOMETHING OR SOMEONE IS KNOCKING AT THE DOOR? THESE ARE AMAZING!
THIRSTY SPACE MONSTERS. WATER! NEED LOTS OF WATER!
RING!!!!
WHAT THE! OH!
HELLO?
YES, THEY ARE PACKED.
I'LL DO MY BEST.

THE GRaND IS A GAMMA RAY AND NEUTRON DETECTOR SPECTROMETER
IT MUST BE MONSTERS. THE PRESIDENT OF THE UNITED STATES OF AMERICA REQUESTS MY PRESENCE AT AN URGENT MEETING AT THE WHITE HOUSE. A CAR IS EN ROUTE TO PICK ME UP.
I NEED TO BORROW YOUR BRAIN. PLEASE GO OVER THE DATA AGAIN. I HAD THE TEAM TURN VISIBLE, INFRARED, AND GRaND TOWARD THE STARS
DESIGNED TO MEASURE ELEMENTAL ABUNDANCES ON THE SURFACE OF VESTA AND CERES.
FOR ONE ORBIT. IF IT'S KLINGONS, THEY WILL BE CLOAKED. LET ME KNOW IF I MISSED ANYTHING. AND HAVE FUN WITH THE PANCAKES.

MANNY GATHERS HIS THINGS TO LEAVE. JOYCE SUDDENLY RECALLS AN UNANSWERED QUESTION.
THIS IS GETTING SCARY.
WHAT DID YOU MEAN ON THE PHONE BY "I'LL DO MY BEST"?
THE PRESIDENT REQUESTED I LEAVE MY BAD JOKES IN LOS ANGELES.
I LIKE THAT WOMAN.

TELL THE KIDS I RAN AWAY FROM HOME SO I WOULDN'T HAVE TO MAKE PANCAKES!
WHERE'S YOUR SUITCASE? I'M PACKING YOUR JOKES! SHE'LL JUST HAVE TO BE DISAPPOINTED!

TWENTY MINUTES LATER, JOYCE ENTERS THEIR BEDROOM AND FINDS MANNY WRITING A NOTE TO EACH CHILD.
DR. DREW'S NOTE TO EACH CHILD READS, "DO NOT TELL THE OTHERS. I LOVE YOU THE MOST!"
YOUR RIDE IS HERE.
THEY CAN WAIT.
THEY CAN WAIT. I GOT TO FIND THE NUMBER OF THE WOMAN WHO PICKED ME UP AT THE AIRPORT.
IN MY SHORT TIME WITH HER, I KNEW SHE WAS THE ONE.
I SAT IN ON YOUR PRESENTATION ON THE INFINITE UNIVERSE.
OUT THERE IS MY TWIN, WHO LOVES HIS WIFE AS MUCH AS I LOVE YOU.
I LOVE YOU MORE.
WHEN MY COPY TELLS HIS INCREDIBLE WIFE, HE LOVES HER MORE THAN LIFE.
HE IS WRONG.

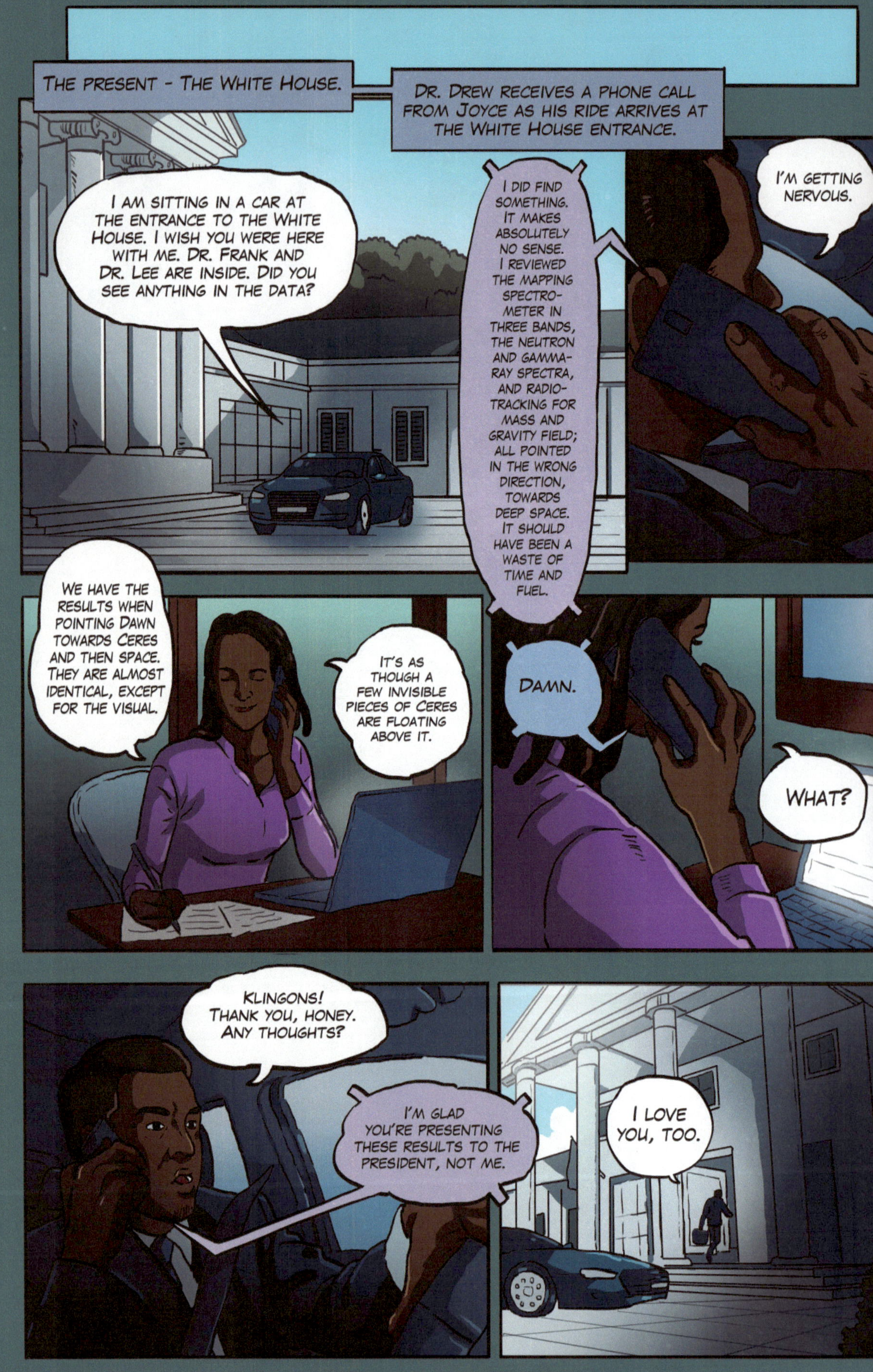

THE PRESENT - THE WHITE HOUSE.
DR. DREW RECEIVES A PHONE CALL FROM JOYCE AS HIS RIDE ARRIVES AT THE WHITE HOUSE ENTRANCE.
I AM SITTING IN A CAR AT THE ENTRANCE TO THE WHITE HOUSE. I WISH YOU WERE HERE WITH ME. DR. FRANK AND DR. LEE ARE INSIDE. DID YOU SEE ANYTHING IN THE DATA?
I DID FIND SOMETHING. IT MAKES ABSOLUTELY NO SENSE. I REVIEWED THE MAPPING SPECTRO-METER IN THREE BANDS, THE NEUTRON AND GAMMA-RAY SPECTRA, AND RADIO-TRACKING FOR MASS AND GRAVITY FIELD; ALL POINTED IN THE WRONG DIRECTION, TOWARDS DEEP SPACE. IT SHOULD HAVE BEEN A WASTE OF TIME AND FUEL.
I'M GETTING NERVOUS.
WE HAVE THE RESULTS WHEN POINTING DAWN TOWARDS CERES AND THEN SPACE. THEY ARE ALMOST IDENTICAL, EXCEPT FOR THE VISUAL.
IT'S AS THOUGH A FEW INVISIBLE PIECES OF CERES ARE FLOATING ABOVE IT.
DAMN.
WHAT?
KLINGONS! THANK YOU, HONEY. ANY THOUGHTS?
I'M GLAD YOU'RE PRESENTING THESE RESULTS TO THE PRESIDENT, NOT ME.
I LOVE YOU, TOO.

A WHITE HOUSE STAFFER ESCORTS DR. DREW TO A LARGE CONFERENCE ROOM IN THE WEST WING, WHERE HE FINDS A GROUP OF PEOPLE, A FEW IN UNIFORM, AND DR. FRANK AND DR. JANE LEE. SHE GREETS DR. DREW WITH A WARM SMILE.

THE PRESIDENT AND HER TEAM WILL JOIN YOU SHORTLY. PLEASE HELP YOURSELF TO WATER OR COFFEE.

PLEASE BE SEATED.

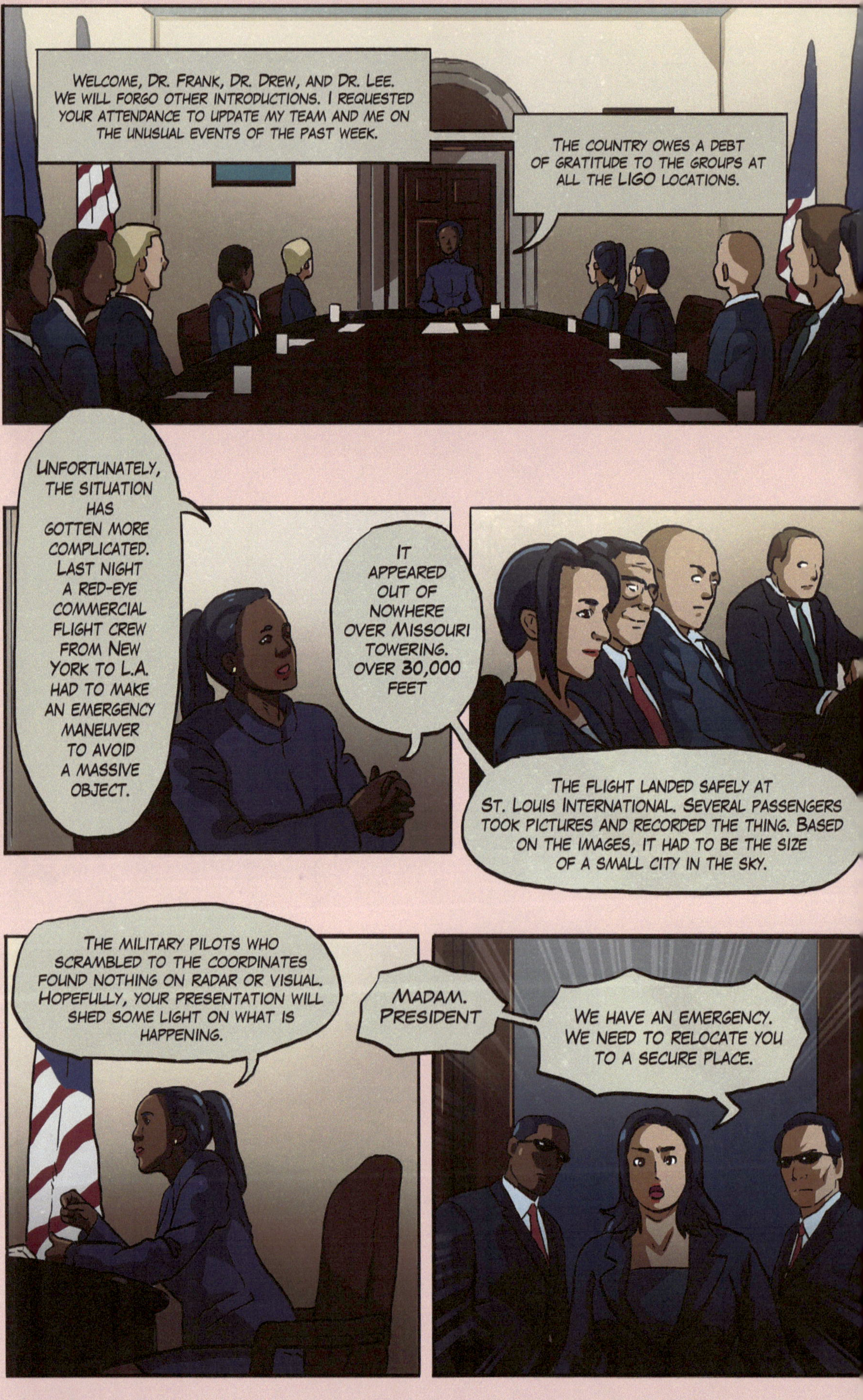

WELCOME, DR. FRANK, DR. DREW, AND DR. LEE. WE WILL FORGO OTHER INTRODUCTIONS. I REQUESTED YOUR ATTENDANCE TO UPDATE MY TEAM AND ME ON THE UNUSUAL EVENTS OF THE PAST WEEK.
THE COUNTRY OWES A DEBT OF GRATITUDE TO THE GROUPS AT ALL THE LIGO LOCATIONS.
UNFORTUNATELY, THE SITUATION HAS GOTTEN MORE COMPLICATED. LAST NIGHT A RED-EYE COMMERCIAL FLIGHT CREW FROM NEW YORK TO L.A. HAD TO MAKE AN EMERGENCY MANEUVER TO AVOID A MASSIVE OBJECT.
IT APPEARED OUT OF NOWHERE OVER MISSOURI TOWERING. OVER 30,000 FEET
THE FLIGHT LANDED SAFELY AT ST. LOUIS INTERNATIONAL. SEVERAL PASSENGERS TOOK PICTURES AND RECORDED THE THING. BASED ON THE IMAGES, IT HAD TO BE THE SIZE OF A SMALL CITY IN THE SKY.
THE MILITARY PILOTS WHO SCRAMBLED TO THE COORDINATES FOUND NOTHING ON RADAR OR VISUAL. HOPEFULLY, YOUR PRESENTATION WILL SHED SOME LIGHT ON WHAT IS HAPPENING.
MADAM. PRESIDENT
WE HAVE AN EMERGENCY. WE NEED TO RELOCATE YOU TO A SECURE PLACE.

STOP! ARE WE UNDER ATTACK? IS THE VICE PRESIDENT SECURE?
THE VICE PRESIDENT IS SECURE.
THEN, FIRST, SECURE THE STAFF AND OUR GUESTS TO A SECURE LOCATION. I WILL JOIN THEM ONCE THE ENTIRE TEAM IS SAFE.
MADAM PRESIDENT. TEAMS ARE SECURING THE ENTIRE WHITE HOUSE STAFF. WE CANNOT ALLOW YOU TO STAY HERE. YOU MUST COME WITH US, PLEASE.
I WANT EVERYONE IN THIS ROOM TO GO WITH ME. GET EVERYONE, AND I MEAN EVERYONE, TO A SAFE PLACE!
MARIA TALK TO ME!
EVERYONE, NOW! FOLLOW THE AGENTS!. HURRY!
SOMEWHERE BENEATH THE WHITE HOUSE, THE THREE SCIENTISTS SIT ALONE IN A CONFERENCE ROOM WHEN A SECRET SERVICE AGENT ENTERS.
PLEASE FOLLOW ME.

EVERYONE IS IN A STATE OF SHOCK, INCLUDING PRESIDENT JAMES.

ON AN ENORMOUS SCREEN IS A BEAUTIFUL SCENE OF OZARK NATIONAL PARK. RISING FROM THE HILLSIDES IS A FIVE-MILE-IN-DIAMETER CYLINDER STRUCTURE RISING FROM THE GROUND, BEYOND THE EARTH'S ATMOSPHERE, AND INTO SPACE.

THERE ARE NO REPORTS OF INJURY IN THE AREA. WE HAVE GROUNDED AIRCRAFT WITHIN A TWO-HUNDRED-MILE RADIUS OF THE STRUCTURE.
THE TOWER IS ON FEDERAL LAND. GOVERNORS AND LOCAL LEADERS ARE REGULARLY UPDATED.
EXCELLENT.
THIS OBJECT JUST, POOF, APPEARED AT THE "EXACT" COORDINATES REPORTED LAST NIGHT BY COMMERCIAL PILOTS BUT COULD NOT BE DETECTED BY OUR PILOTS.
WHAT TIME DID IT APPEAR?
THE FIRST SIGHTING WAS EXACTLY ONE HOUR AGO. WHY?
I RECEIVED A CALL JUST BEFORE OUR MEETING, MADAM PRESIDENT.
DO YOU BELIEVE THERE'S A CONNECTION?
WE BELIEVE THIS STRUCTURE ANNOUNCES THEIR ARRIVAL.
WE RECORDED ANOTHER GRAVITATIONAL WAVE ABOUT THE SAME TIME THIS STRUCTURE APPEARED.
NO MORE HIDING. IT STARTS.

Dr. Drew speaks to the military officer, who is visibly irritated
I strongly suggest that the Air Force pilots who scrambled to the coordinates have a thorough physical and more questioning.
We have already questioned them at length. They are two of our best.
Dr. Drew continues making his case, still calm but firm.
Sir, I understand. Please indulge me for a moment. We have visual proof that the object was there last night
Your pilots flew their planes in the exact area where the structure, the size of a city and reaching beyond the sky, is still standing and they made it safely back to base with no sighting.
That does not add up!
Sir, I have important information I would like to share with your permission.
Madam President?
Please continue.

I ALSO HAVE AN UPDATE ON THE FIRST THREE GRAVITATIONAL WAVES THAT ORIGINATED NEAR CERES. WE TURNED THE DAWN SPACECRAFT AWAY FROM CERES TOWARDS DEEP SPACE FOR SEVERAL ORBITS AND CONTINUED OUR TESTS.
BASED ON THE DATA WE WILL PROVIDE, WE DETECTED THE POSSIBILITY OF THREE LARGE OBJECTS HOVERING ABOVE CERES.
OBJECTS?
POSSIBLY, SPACESHIPS OF SOME TYPE, CLOAKED SPACESHIPS.
YOU CANNOT BE SERIOUS. SPACESHIPS!
WE ALL SEE IT BUT COULDN'T POSSIBLY BUILD IT. A HERO PILOT BARELY AVOIDED IT LAST NIGHT. BEFORE LAST NIGHT, NO ONE REPORTED SEEING OR HEARING IT UNDER CONSTRUCTION. NOTHING EVEN CLOSE TO THIS HAS EVER EXISTED IN THE HISTORY OF THE WORLD.
YOUR BEST PILOTS COULDN'T FIND IT. WITHOUT OUR MILITARY, OUR SPY NETWORKS, OR EVEN A FARMER DISCOVERING IT, WHOEVER PUT IT THERE COULD BE IN THIS ROOM RIGHT NOW, AND WE WOULD NOT KNOW IT.
I WANT DR. DREW AND THE LIGO TEAM TO HAVE UNRESTRICTED ACCESS TO THE PILOTS DURING THE INTERVIEWS.
PLEASE EXCUSE ME, MADAM PRESIDENT. PLEASE REQUEST A DETAILED FLIGHT TIME VS. FUEL CONSUMPTION REPORT FOR EACH SCRAMBLED PLANE.

A SECOND OFFICER INTERRUPTS THE PRESIDENT WITH DISTURBING NEW IMAGES.
MADAM PRESIDENT.
PLEASE WATCH.
MORE STRUCTURES ARE APPEARING OUT OF NOWHERE.
MAINE

OHIO

THE GULF OF MEXICO

NORTH CAROLINA COAST

NEW YORK

THE CHESAPEAKE BAY.

EVERYONE IS SHOCKED TO SEE
HOW CLOSE THE FINAL STRUCTURE
IS TO THE U.S. CAPITOL.

THE
CHESAPEAKE
BAY! MADAM
PRESIDENT,
THAT'S
LESS THAN 50
MILES AWAY!

PRESIDENT JAMES ADDRESSES DR. DREW, DR. JANE LEE, AND DR. FRANK.
I WILL ADDRESS THE NATION AND UPDATE WORLD LEADERS. THANK YOU. NO PRESS.
OUR STAFF WILL TAKE YOU TO YOUR HOTEL. YOU WILL HAVE 24-HOUR SECURITY AND A DIRECT LINK TO MY STAFF.
PRESIDENT JAMES STOPS THEM AS THEY EXIT.
THOSE TOWERS ARE FIVE MILES IN DIAMETER AND RISE INTO SPACE. I LOVE GEOLOGY. I GOT A "C" IN PHYSICS. STILL, EVEN I KNOW WE DO NOT POSSESS THE TECHNOLOGY OR MATERIALS TO BUILD THEM.
THEY WOULD BE TOO HEAVY FOR THE EARTH'S CRUST TO SUPPORT. THEY SHOULD BE SINKING INTO THE PLANET. AM I CORRECT?
MADAM PRESIDENT, YOU ARE CORRECT.
THANK YOU. I AM ORDERING ALL FLIGHTS GROUNDED WITHIN 200MILES OF THESE THINGS AND MILITARY RECON FLIGHTS AROUND THEM 24/7
WHO KNOWS WHERE THE NEXT ONE WILL POP UP?

A LOCAL NEW YORK NEWS CREW IS ABOARD A HIGH-SPEED BOAT, RUSHING TO GET THE FIRST LIVE REPORT FROM THE TOWER IN THE WATERS OFF NEW YORK.
I HAVE BAD NEWS.
WE'VE BEEN AT FULL THROTTLE FOR A HALF HOUR, AND WE'RE GETTING NO CLOSER TO THE STRUCTURE. DO YOUR REPORT FROM HERE, OR I'LL RETURN TO THE DOCK. WE'RE RUNNING LOW ON FUEL.
-OHIO-
A COUPLE RACES TO BE THE FIRST TO TOUCH THE MASSIVE TOWER
HONEY, CAN WE STOP? WE'VE BEEN RIDING FOR MORE THAN AN HOUR. I WANT TO CHECK MY GPS.
DAMN! NO WAY!
WHAT!
WE'RE NO CLOSER THAN WE WERE AN HOUR AGO!

THE PRESENT

SPACE, NEAR THE MOON.
TIMESHIP ENCOUNTER HAS ARRIVED.

MEMBERS OF M.O.M. WATCH
A THREE-DIMENSIONAL VIEW OF
PRESIDENT JAMES'S MEETING.

IT'S
TIME.

MR. D AND
NEUTRINA ARE
APPROACHING
THE SUN.

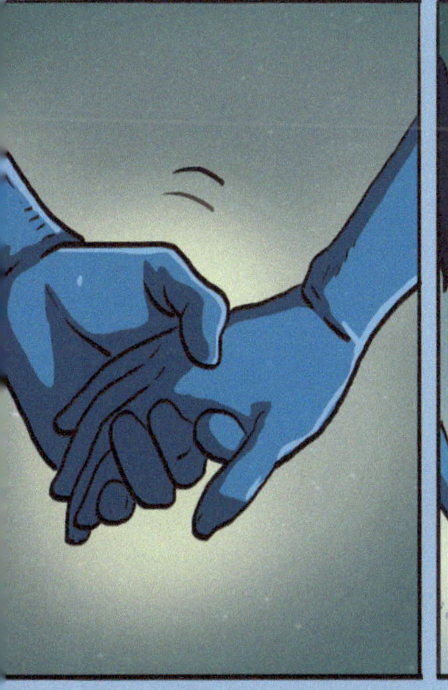

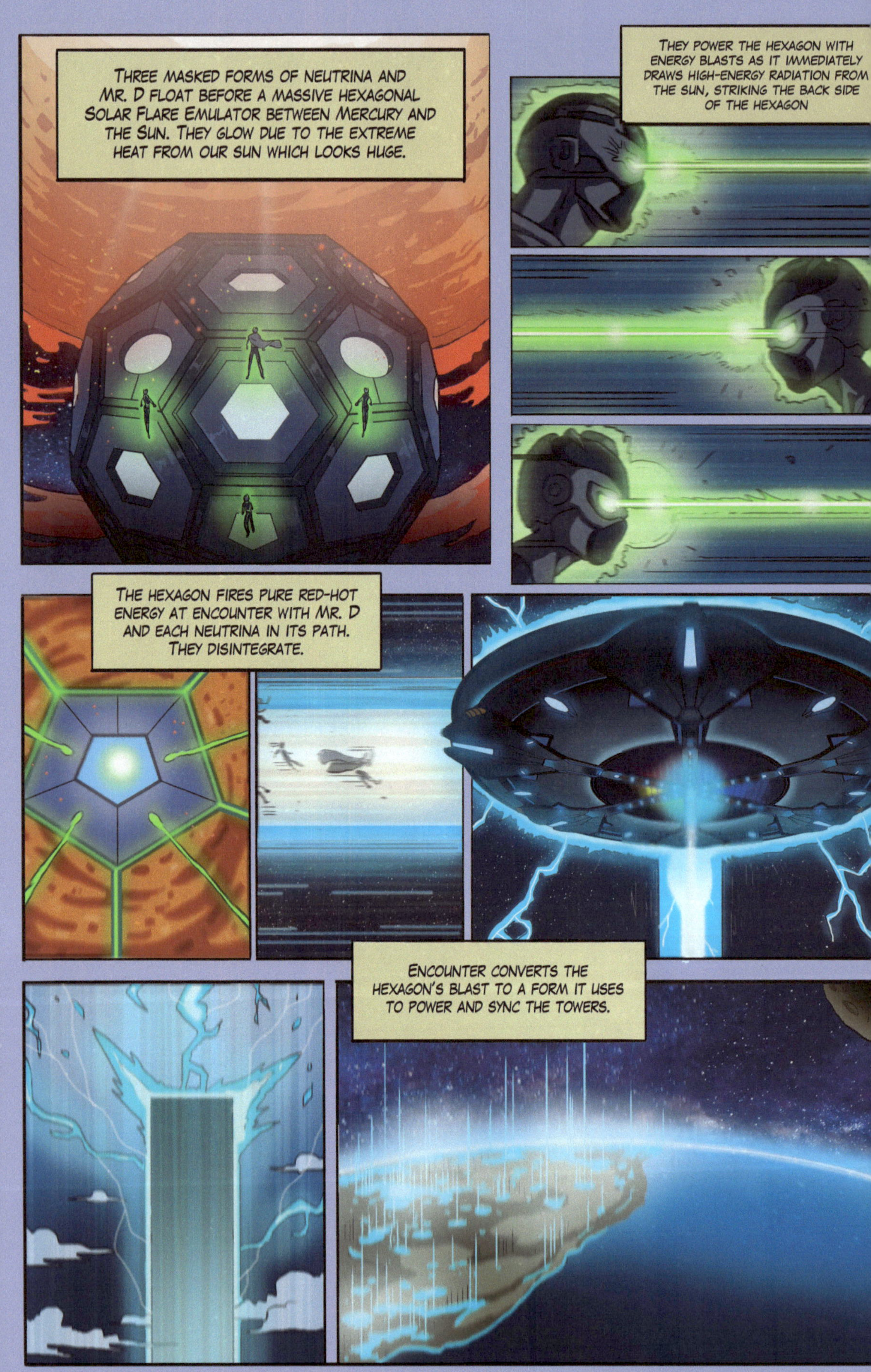

THREE MASKED FORMS OF NEUTRINA AND MR. D FLOAT BEFORE A MASSIVE HEXAGONAL SOLAR FLARE EMULATOR BETWEEN MERCURY AND THE SUN. THEY GLOW DUE TO THE EXTREME HEAT FROM OUR SUN WHICH LOOKS HUGE.
THEY POWER THE HEXAGON WITH ENERGY BLASTS AS IT IMMEDIATELY DRAWS HIGH-ENERGY RADIATION FROM THE SUN, STRIKING THE BACK SIDE OF THE HEXAGON
THE HEXAGON FIRES PURE RED-HOT ENERGY AT ENCOUNTER WITH MR. D AND EACH NEUTRINA IN ITS PATH. THEY DISINTEGRATE.
ENCOUNTER CONVERTS THE HEXAGON'S BLAST TO A FORM IT USES TO POWER AND SYNC THE TOWERS.

POWERED BY THE SUN, ENCOUNTER SYNCS WITH THE SEVEN TOWERS, PRODUCING AN INVISIBLE FORCE FIELD OF PURE ENERGY COVERING THE EASTERN U.S. M.O.M. KNOWS MicroV IS HIDING THERE. NOW, THERE IS NO ESCAPE.
-LATER-
MR. D AND NEUTRINA REAPPEAR UNHARMED, FLOATING IN SPACE, LOOKING DOWN AT HOW THE FORCE FIELD MAKES NIGHT LIGHTS ALONG THE EASTERN U.S. LOOK BLUE FROM SPACE.

A SMALL GROUP OF SENIOR CITIZENS RUNS PAST TWO SHOCKED YOUNG ATHLETES IN A PARK, WAVING AND SMILING.
DID YOU SEE THAT?
YEAH! WHAT'S WITH THE WAVING AND BEING NICE?
NO! I RUN PAST THEM EVERY DAY. THEY NEVER SPEAK. THEY NEVER RUN. NEVER!
NEW YORK-NEWARK NEWS NETWORK METEOROLOGIST GIVES DAILY AIR QUALITY RESULTS.
WELL, AT LEAST WE KNOW ONE POSITIVE RESULT OF THIS THING APPEARING OUT OF NOWHERE. TODAY, WE HAVE THE CLEANEST AIR ON RECORD,
BUT THE QUESTION REMAINS: AT WHAT COST?
BREAKING NEWS
LIVE
N.N
u.s. one positive result of this thing appearing out of nowhere
MOST SIGNIFICANT HISTORICAL EVENT EVER
A HIGH SCHOOL PRINCIPAL SITS AT HIS DESK AS FIVE TEACHERS ENTER.
FIGHT? HAVE YOU BEEN OUT OF THE OFFICE TODAY?
SNN BREAKING NEWS!
OK. PLEASE TAKE A DEEP BREATH BEFORE WE DISCUSS WHATEVER BRINGS YOU HERE, NOT FIGHT.
THE STUDENTS, WOW! THEY!
THEY ARE FANTASTIC TODAY! THEY ARE!
PRESIDENT JAMES WILL ADDRESS THE NATION FROM THE OVAL OFFICE TODAY ON THE MOST SIGNIFICANT HISTORICAL EVENT EVER.

PRESENT
M.O.M. MEMBERS VIEW THE FORCE FIELD FROM ABOARD ENCOUNTER.
IT IS TIME FOR A COURTESY MEETING WITH PRESIDENT JAMES.
PRESENT - WHITE HOUSE OVAL OFFICE - PRESIDENT JAMES WORKS AT HER DESK.
SHE LOOKS UP TO SEE TRUTH, HARRIET, AND THE THREE LUCYS. SHE IS SURPRISED, NOT FRIGHTENED, BY FIVE BEAUTIFUL WOMEN STANDING IN HER OFFICE WITHOUT HEARING THE DOOR OPEN OR ANYONE ESCORTING THEM IN.
I'M GOING TO CALL IN MY CHIEF OF STAFF.
IS THAT OK?
MARIA, MAY I SEE YOU FOR A MOMENT?
YES, MADAM PRESIDENT.
COS MARIA SANCHEZ ENTERS FROM THE ADJACENT OFFICE AND IS STARTLED TO SEE THE VISITORS.
MARIA.
MADAM PRESIDENT! I'M SORRY. I WAS NOT AWARE YOU HAD AN UNSCHEDULED MEETING.
THAT'S BECAUSE I DON'T.

PRESIDENT JAMES TURNS TO HER UNINVITED GUESTS.
YOU WALKED INTO THE OVAL OFFICE UNDETECTED. IT MUST HAVE BEEN A WALK IN THE PARK COMPARED TO SECRETLY CONSTRUCTING THE TOWERS.
AM I CORRECT THAT YOU BUILT THE STRUCTURES?
YES. MADAM PRESIDENT, WE DID. I AM LUCY STONE. PLEASE LET ME INTRODUCE EVERYONE. FIRST, LUCY COLMAN.
LUCY COLMAN
WE ARE HONORED TO MEET YOU, MADAM PRESIDENT.
LUCY STANTON.
LUCY STANTON.
AN HONOR, MADAM PRESIDENT.
SOJOURNER TRUTH
SOJOURNER TRUTH.
HONORED, MADAM RESIDENT.
MADAM PRESIDENT. WE SPEAK FOR AMERICA. WE ARE HONORED TO BE IN YOUR PRESENCE.
HARRIET TUBMAN
OUR LEADER, HARRIET TUBMAN.

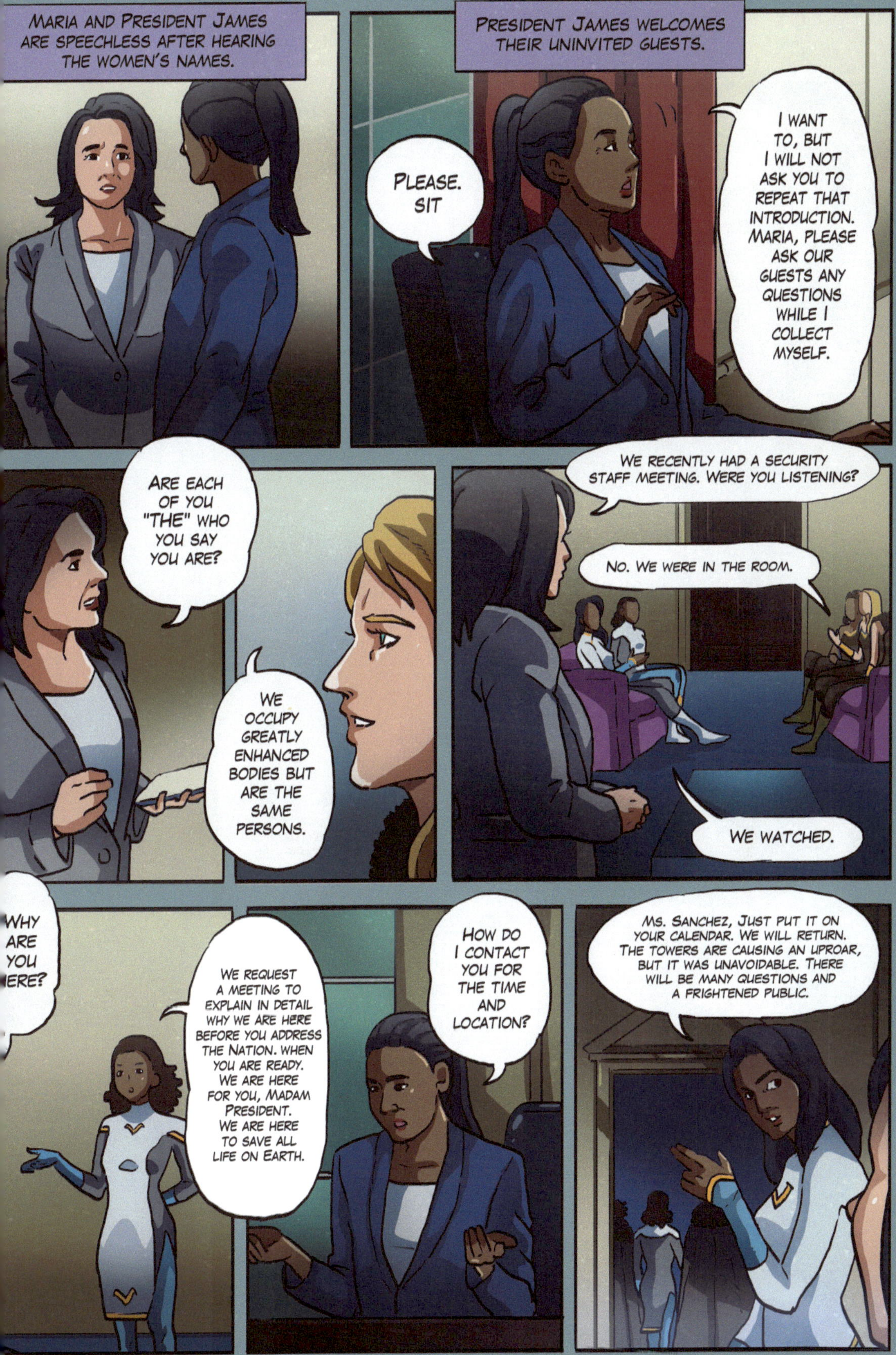

MARIA AND PRESIDENT JAMES ARE SPEECHLESS AFTER HEARING THE WOMEN'S NAMES.

PRESIDENT JAMES WELCOMES THEIR UNINVITED GUESTS.

PLEASE. SIT

I WANT TO, BUT I WILL NOT ASK YOU TO REPEAT THAT INTRODUCTION. MARIA, PLEASE ASK OUR GUESTS ANY QUESTIONS WHILE I COLLECT MYSELF.

ARE EACH OF YOU "THE" WHO YOU SAY YOU ARE?

WE OCCUPY GREATLY ENHANCED BODIES BUT ARE THE SAME PERSONS.

WE RECENTLY HAD A SECURITY STAFF MEETING. WERE YOU LISTENING?

NO. WE WERE IN THE ROOM.

WE WATCHED.

WHY ARE YOU HERE?

WE REQUEST A MEETING TO EXPLAIN IN DETAIL WHY WE ARE HERE BEFORE YOU ADDRESS THE NATION. WHEN YOU ARE READY. WE ARE HERE FOR YOU, MADAM PRESIDENT. WE ARE HERE TO SAVE ALL LIFE ON EARTH.

HOW DO I CONTACT YOU FOR THE TIME AND LOCATION?

MS. SANCHEZ, JUST PUT IT ON YOUR CALENDAR. WE WILL RETURN. THE TOWERS ARE CAUSING AN UPROAR, BUT IT WAS UNAVOIDABLE. THERE WILL BE MANY QUESTIONS AND A FRIGHTENED PUBLIC.

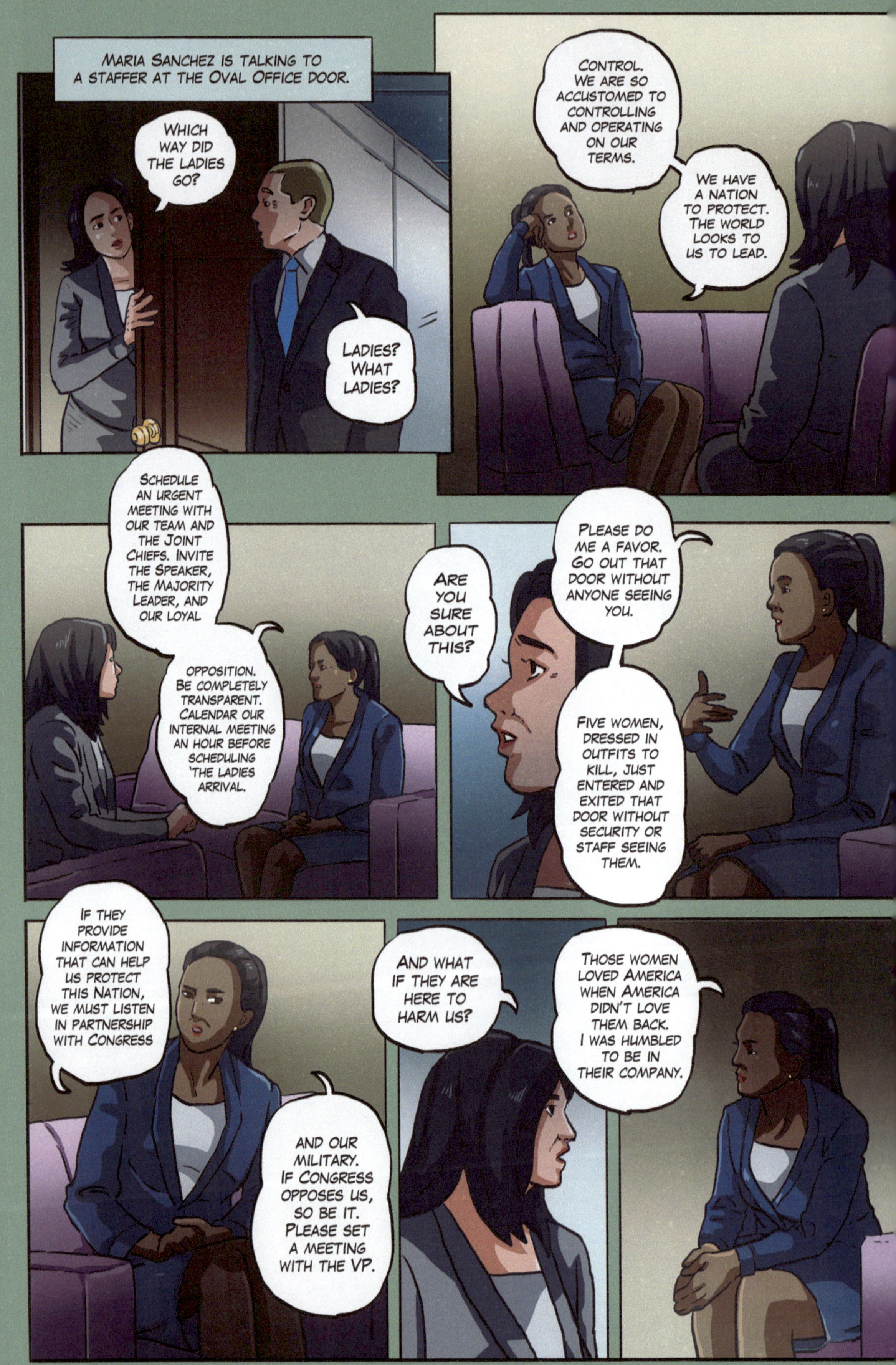

MARIA SANCHEZ IS TALKING TO A STAFFER AT THE OVAL OFFICE DOOR.
WHICH WAY DID THE LADIES GO?
LADIES? WHAT LADIES?
CONTROL. WE ARE SO ACCUSTOMED TO CONTROLLING AND OPERATING ON OUR TERMS.
WE HAVE A NATION TO PROTECT. THE WORLD LOOKS TO US TO LEAD.
SCHEDULE AN URGENT MEETING WITH OUR TEAM AND THE JOINT CHIEFS. INVITE THE SPEAKER, THE MAJORITY LEADER, AND OUR LOYAL
OPPOSITION. BE COMPLETELY TRANSPARENT. CALENDAR OUR INTERNAL MEETING AN HOUR BEFORE SCHEDULING 'THE LADIES ARRIVAL.
ARE YOU SURE ABOUT THIS?
PLEASE DO ME A FAVOR. GO OUT THAT DOOR WITHOUT ANYONE SEEING YOU.
FIVE WOMEN, DRESSED IN OUTFITS TO KILL, JUST ENTERED AND EXITED THAT DOOR WITHOUT SECURITY OR STAFF SEEING THEM.
IF THEY PROVIDE INFORMATION THAT CAN HELP US PROTECT THIS NATION, WE MUST LISTEN IN PARTNERSHIP WITH CONGRESS
AND OUR MILITARY. IF CONGRESS OPPOSES US, SO BE IT. PLEASE SET A MEETING WITH THE VP.
AND WHAT IF THEY ARE HERE TO HARM US?
THOSE WOMEN LOVED AMERICA WHEN AMERICA DIDN'T LOVE THEM BACK. I WAS HUMBLED TO BE IN THEIR COMPANY.

LOS ANGELES
JOYCE SITS IN THE STANDS WITH TOSHA AND COBY ON THE PHONE WITH MANNY WHILE AT KHALID'S BASKETBALL GAME.
ALL YOU SEE ON THE NEWS ARE THOSE TOWERS TO SPACE. PARENTS ARE SCARED. THE KIDS ARE CLUELESS, LIFE AS USUAL. HOW ARE YOU?
JOYCE LISTENS TO MANNY'S REPLY.
SHE'S SITTING NEXT TO ME. WE CHANGED HER NAME. SHE THINKS SHE'S JEWELL LOYD. THE COACH SAT HER TO KEEP THE SCORE RESPECTABLE.
SHE TRIED JUST TO SET THE OTHER GIRLS UP, AND SHE DID, BUT THE SHOTS WERE THERE, AND SHE TOOK THEM, AND SHE KEPT MAKING THEM.

JOYCE GIVES THE PHONE TO TOSHA.
COME HOME!
TOSHA PAUSES WHILE DR. DREW IS TALKING.
WE'RE SCARED.
THEY WERE FRIENDLY AND TRIED HARD, BUT WE WERE FASTER AND MORE EXPERIENCED.
TOSHA SMILES WHILE DR. DREW IS TALKING.
MOM FILMED THE GAME. WE CAN WATCH IT TOGETHER.
STOP IT, DADDY!
JOYCE WANTS TO KNOW WHAT CAUSED TOSHA TO RAISE HER VOICE.
WHAT DID HE SAY? DID HE TELL A JOKE?
YES. I TOLD HIM ABOUT THIS CUTE BOY, SO HE WANTED TO INVITE HIM TO WATCH MY GAME WITH US.

JOYCE CONTINUES HER PHONE CONVERSATION WITH MANNY WHILE WATCHING KHALID'S BASKETBALL GAME.
WE'RE AHEAD BY THIRTY. HE'S PLAYING OUT OF HIS MIND. I BELIEVE THERE ARE SCOUTS HERE TO WATCH HIM. HE'S JUST IN MIDDLE SCHOOL!

CAN I SAY SOMETHING, PLEASE?

DADDY!
HE'S HAVING A GOOD GAME - GREAT PASSING- FIVE THREES IN THE FIRST HALF - SCARY HANDLES! BUT GOT TO BE MORE SELFISH - JUST KIDDING!
SCOUTS ARE HERE! COBY GOT TWO LETTERS TODAY, DIVISION I.
TOSHA GIVES THE PHONE TO COBY.

COBY TALKS TO MANNY WHILE TOSHA LAUGHS IN THE BACKGROUND.
SHE HAS A BIG MOUTH, DAD.
NOT TWO LETTERS; I GOT THREE.
I WAS GOING TO SURPRISE YOU, BUT.
YOU'LL BE IMPRESSED WHEN YOU SEE THE NAMES, BUT I'M STILL' WAITING TO HEAR FROM YOUR ALMA MATA. I WANT TO STAY CLOSE TO HOME.
I LOVE YOU, TOO.
WHEN WILL YOU BE COMING HOME?
SOMETHING BIG MUST BE COMING FOR THAT TO HAPPEN.
TAKE CARE OF YOURSELF. LOVE YOU.
NO. YOU DO NOT.
I LOVE YOU MORE, NOW GET TO WORK.
IT'S A TIE.
TIES GO TO THE WOMEN.
JOYCE AND TOSHA HIGH-FIVE AS KHALID MAKES ANOTHER THREE.

SUNSET
CASCADE CAVES KENTUCKY.
EASTERN KENTUCKY
THOUSANDS OF BATS FLY FROM THE CAVE WALLS PAST THE 30-FOOT-TALL CRYSTAL FLOATING ABOVE A STREAM OF WATER FLOWING TO THE ENORMOUS CAVE OPENING.
THE CRYSTAL EMITS ENERGY BEAMS, STRIKING HUNDREDS, SENDING THEM INTO THE SHALLOW WATER FLOWING THROUGH THE CAVE.
THE BATS APPEAR LIFELESS, FLOATING IN THE WATER.

LIKE VAMPIRES OF LEGEND, MicroV NEEDS AWARENESS OF ITS SURROUNDINGS AND PROTECTION WHILE IT SLEEPS.
MONSTER BATS WITH 150-FOOT WINGSPANS FLY OUT INTO THE EVENING SKY, POSSESSING POWERS BEYOND OUR MILITARY'S MOST ADVANCED TECHNOLOGY AND FIREPOWER, TRANSMITTING DATA BACK TO MicroV.

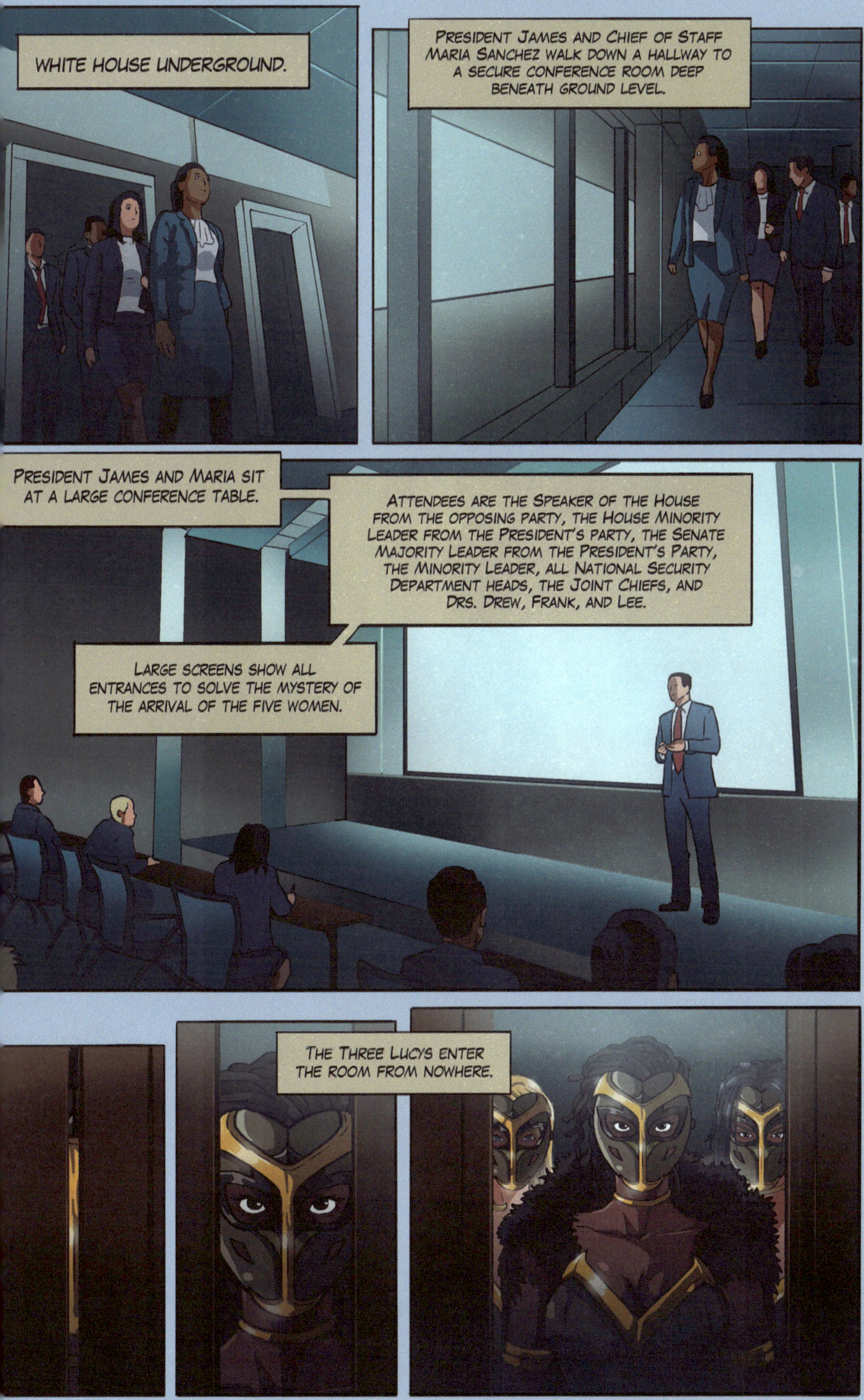

WHITE HOUSE UNDERGROUND.

PRESIDENT JAMES AND CHIEF OF STAFF MARIA SANCHEZ WALK DOWN A HALLWAY TO A SECURE CONFERENCE ROOM DEEP BENEATH GROUND LEVEL.

PRESIDENT JAMES AND MARIA SIT AT A LARGE CONFERENCE TABLE.

ATTENDEES ARE THE SPEAKER OF THE HOUSE FROM THE OPPOSING PARTY, THE HOUSE MINORITY LEADER FROM THE PRESIDENT'S PARTY, THE SENATE MAJORITY LEADER FROM THE PRESIDENT'S PARTY, THE MINORITY LEADER, ALL NATIONAL SECURITY DEPARTMENT HEADS, THE JOINT CHIEFS, AND DRS. DREW, FRANK, AND LEE.

LARGE SCREENS SHOW ALL ENTRANCES TO SOLVE THE MYSTERY OF THE ARRIVAL OF THE FIVE WOMEN.

THE THREE LUCYS ENTER THE ROOM FROM NOWHERE.

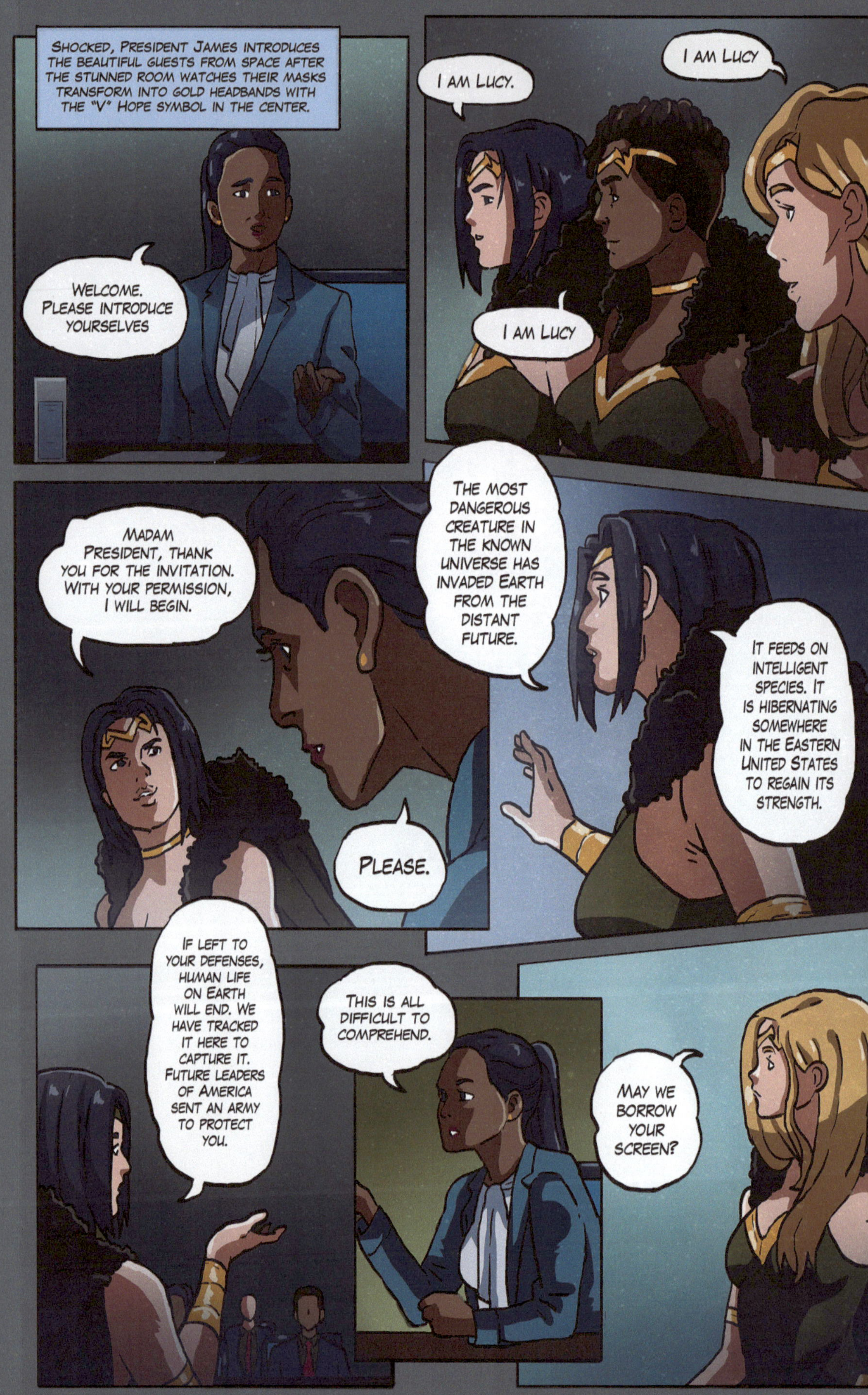

Shocked, President James introduces the beautiful guests from space after the stunned room watches their masks transform into gold headbands with the "V" Hope symbol in the center.
Welcome. Please introduce yourselves
I am Lucy.
I am Lucy
I am Lucy
Madam President, thank you for the invitation. With your permission, I will begin.
The most dangerous creature in the known universe has invaded Earth from the distant future.
It feeds on intelligent species. It is hibernating somewhere in the Eastern United States to regain its strength.
Please.
If left to your defenses, human life on Earth will end. We have tracked it here to capture it. Future leaders of America sent an army to protect you.
This is all difficult to comprehend.
May we borrow your screen?

APPEARING ON THE LARGE CONFERENCE ROOM SCREEN - A PANORAMIC VIEW OF A FUTURISTIC CITY ON A DISTANT PLANET 30,000 YEARS INTO THE FUTURE.
IT'S STRANGE TALKING TO YOU FROM HERE, BUT YOU ARE HERE WITH ME, SEEING THE RESULT OF THIS CREATURE'S EVIL. THEY CALLED IT MICROV.
THERE WERE MILLIONS OF THEM DESTROYING PLANETS THROUGHOUT THE GALAXY 20,000 YEARS INTO OUR FUTURE.
EVERYONE IN THE ROOM SEES THEMSELVES ON THE SCREEN, WALKING DOWN THE CENTER OF A LONG CITY STREET, LOOKING AROUND FOR ANY SIGNS OF LIFE. PRESIDENT JAMES SPEAKS TO THE GROUP, INCLUDING HERSELF, FROM THE SCREEN.
THEY ARE INVISIBLE LIKE A VIRUS, ONLY WITH THE EXCEPTIONAL INTELLECT THEY GAINED FROM THEIR VICTIMS.
OUR DESCENDANTS DESTROYED ALL OF THEM EXCEPT ONE, THEIR LEADER. NOW, MICROV HAS TRAVELED BACK IN TIME TO KILL US.
EVERYONE IS CONFUSED ABOUT SEEING THEMSELVES ON THE SCREEN AND SEEING EVERYTHING FROM THE POINT OF VIEW OF THEIR SCREEN IMAGES.

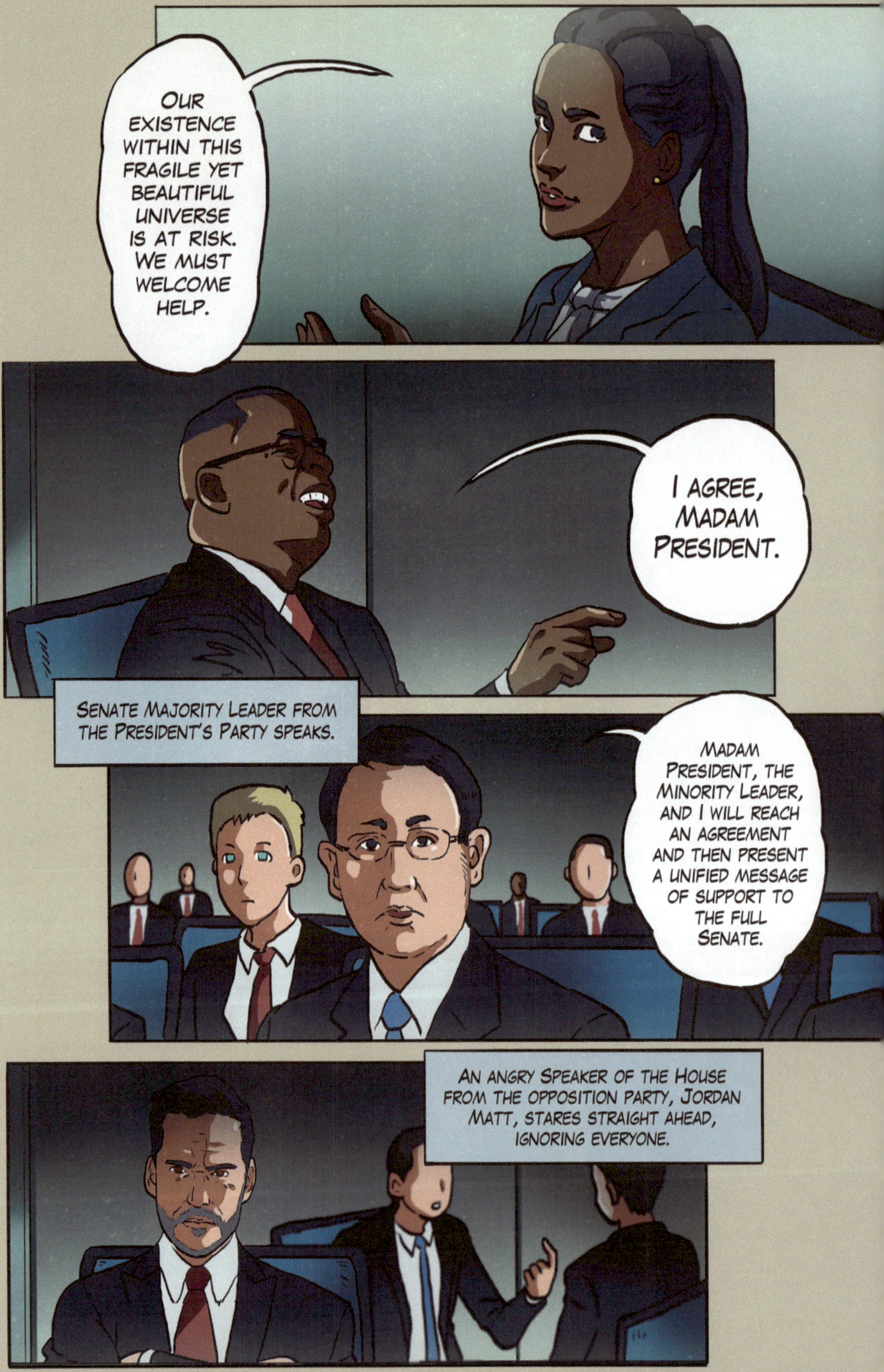

SENATE MAJORITY LEADER FROM THE PRESIDENT'S PARTY SPEAKS.

AN ANGRY SPEAKER OF THE HOUSE FROM THE OPPOSITION PARTY, JORDAN MATT, STARES STRAIGHT AHEAD, IGNORING EVERYONE.

AN AGITATED SPEAKER OF THE HOUSE FROM THE OPPOSITION PARTY ADDRESSES PRESIDENT JAMES.
MADAM PRESIDENT.
RESPECTFULLY, THIS IS RIDICULOUS!
THE SPEAKER OF THE HOUS TURNS TO THE LUCYS.
AND WHAT IS YOUR ROLE IN CAPTURING THIS CREATURE?
WE ARE THE ARMY SENT TO PROTECT YOU.

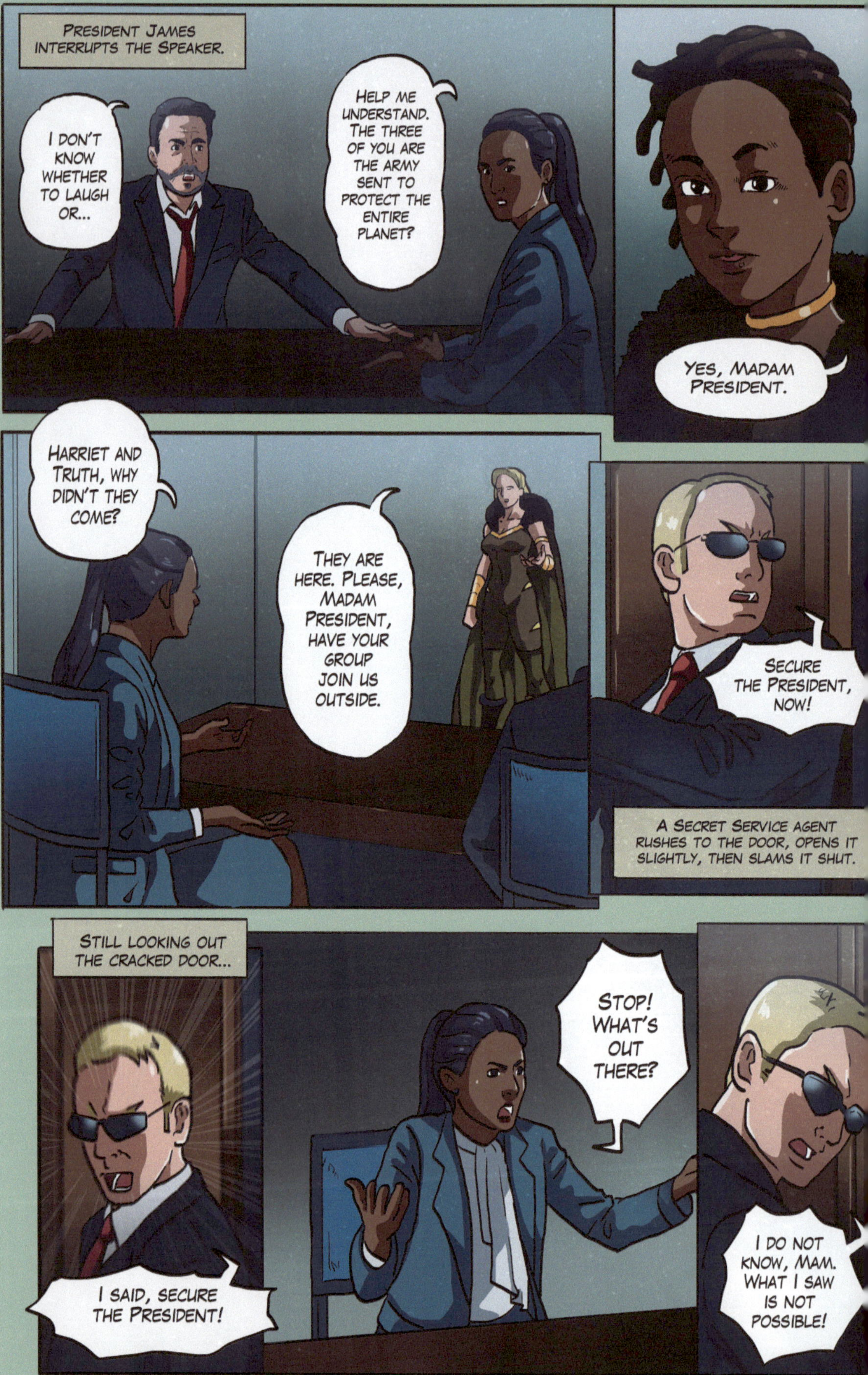

PRESIDENT JAMES INTERRUPTS THE SPEAKER.
I DON'T KNOW WHETHER TO LAUGH OR...
HELP ME UNDERSTAND. THE THREE OF YOU ARE THE ARMY SENT TO PROTECT THE ENTIRE PLANET?
YES, MADAM PRESIDENT.
HARRIET AND TRUTH, WHY DIDN'T THEY COME?
THEY ARE HERE. PLEASE, MADAM PRESIDENT, HAVE YOUR GROUP JOIN US OUTSIDE.
SECURE THE PRESIDENT, NOW!
A SECRET SERVICE AGENT RUSHES TO THE DOOR, OPENS IT SLIGHTLY, THEN SLAMS IT SHUT.
STILL LOOKING OUT THE CRACKED DOOR...
STOP! WHAT'S OUT THERE?
I SAID, SECURE THE PRESIDENT!
I DO NOT KNOW, MAM. WHAT I SAW IS NOT POSSIBLE!

DR. DREW AND A SECRET SERVICE AGENT VOLUNTEER TO FOLLOW THE LUCYS.
DR. DREW AND THE SS AGENT FOLLOW THE THREE LUCYS OUT THE DOOR.
WITH YOUR PERMISSION, MADAM PRESIDENT. ALLOW ME.
I WILL GO WITH HIM, MADAM.
PRESIDENT JAMES AND OTHERS SIT QUIETLY, WATCHING THE DOOR.
DR. DREW AND THE S.S. AGENT RE-ENTER. DR. DREW IS SMILING.
MADAM PRESIDENT, YOU HAVE GOT TO SEE THIS!
PRESIDENT JAMES AND THE ENTIRE GROUP EXIT.

THEY EXIT A SLIDING DOOR FROM A MASSIVE CURVED WALL INTO A VAST CURVED HALL THAT GOES ON FOR MILES. IT HAS A CURVED OUTER WALL.
THEY ARE ON A PLATFORM BETWEEN A TOWER AND AN INNER TOWER THEY UNKNOWINGLY EXITED. HARRIET AND M.O.M. MEMBERS GREET PRESIDENT JAMES, WHO IS WALKING FAR AHEAD OF THE GROUP, UNAFRAID.
MADAM PRESIDENT. YOU HAVE GREETED US WITH KINDNESS. WE KNEW YOU WOULD NEED HELP GETTING OTHERS TO TAKE YOU SERIOUSLY.
I HAVE SO MANY QUESTIONS. HOW IS THIS POSSIBLE? WAIT! ALL THIS ISN'T POSSIBLE! WHO ARE YOU? ARE YOU THE LEADER OF THIS OPERATION?
NO, BUT WE ARE OF ONE VISION. WE ARE MOTHERS OF MEN. WE SERVE THE CITIZENS OF AMERICA, EARTH, AND THE UNIVERSE OF NATIONS. WE, TOO, ARE GUESTS. YOU HAVE NOT MET MR. D. YOU WILL WHEN THE TIME IS RIGHT.
A STILL IRRITATED SPEAKER OF THE HOUSE, JORDAN MATT, POINTS UP AT AN UNSEEN OBJECT.
MR. D? AND WHAT THE HELL IS THAT?

WE SEE A GIGANTIC FUTURE FLAG OF AMERICA ON THE INNER TOWER WALL TOWERING ABOVE THE GROUP.
E PLURIBUS UNUM
THAT, SIR, IS THE AMERICAN FLAG.

A PERPLEXED SENATE MAJORITY LEADER APPROACHES HARRIET.
IN SUPPORT OF PRESIDENT JAMES, WE FELT IT NECESSARY WE SHARE.
VALUES • VIRTUE • VICTORY
QUAL VALUE FOR EVERY LIFE
WHERE ARE WE?
SO, TO ANSWER YOUR QUESTION.
WE WERE IN A SECURE ROOM BENEATH THE WHITE HOUSE A FEW MINUTES AGO.
HARRIET WALKS THE GROUP TOWARDS THE MASSIVE, BLANK WALL THAT SLOWLY BECOMES TRANSPARENT.
LOOK.
THE OUTER WALL OPENS TO REVEAL THEY ARE STANDING 30,000 FEET IN THE SKY ON AN OBSERVATION DECK OF THE TOWER IN THE CHESAPEAKE BAY AS THUNDERSTORMS OCCUR IN THE DISTANT CLOUDS BELOW.

House Speaker Jordan Matt stares angrily at the American flag while the group enjoys the scenic view.
Chief of Staff Maria Sanchez notices the Speaker's angry obsession with the flag.
President James quietly speaks to Harriet while enjoying the view.
Harriet, I have no doubt you brought us here to make a point. So, please know - point made. Whatever is out there seeking to destroy us has a formidable foe in you.
The three Lucys. Are they your entire army?
Yes, and consider yourself fortunate to have them on your side.
Thank you and the mysterious Mr. D, who designed all this.
Harriet turns to President James.
Madam President, we know you have much to discuss with your team, America, and the leaders of other countries. So, in anticipation of your many questions, allow us to share more.
Please do.
VALUES • VIRTUE •
"EQUAL VALUE FOR
Speaker of the House Matt is now studying the Hope Symbol. He is not pleased.

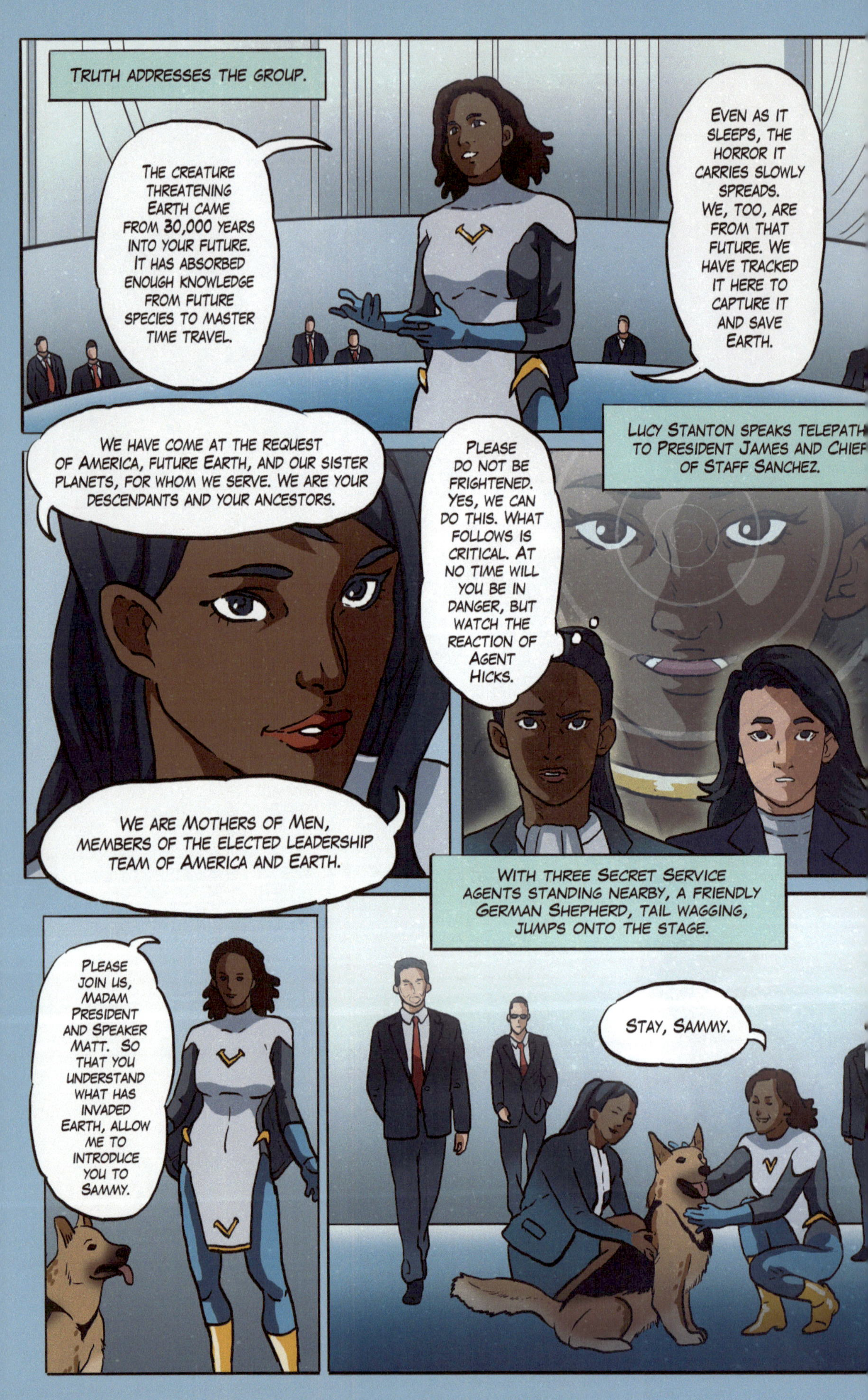

TRUTH ADDRESSES THE GROUP.
THE CREATURE THREATENING EARTH CAME FROM 30,000 YEARS INTO YOUR FUTURE. IT HAS ABSORBED ENOUGH KNOWLEDGE FROM FUTURE SPECIES TO MASTER TIME TRAVEL.
EVEN AS IT SLEEPS, THE HORROR IT CARRIES SLOWLY SPREADS. WE, TOO, ARE FROM THAT FUTURE. WE HAVE TRACKED IT HERE TO CAPTURE IT AND SAVE EARTH.
WE HAVE COME AT THE REQUEST OF AMERICA, FUTURE EARTH, AND OUR SISTER PLANETS, FOR WHOM WE SERVE. WE ARE YOUR DESCENDANTS AND YOUR ANCESTORS.
PLEASE DO NOT BE FRIGHTENED. YES, WE CAN DO THIS. WHAT FOLLOWS IS CRITICAL. AT NO TIME WILL YOU BE IN DANGER, BUT WATCH THE REACTION OF AGENT HICKS.
LUCY STANTON SPEAKS TELEPATH TO PRESIDENT JAMES AND CHIEF OF STAFF SANCHEZ.
WE ARE MOTHERS OF MEN, MEMBERS OF THE ELECTED LEADERSHIP TEAM OF AMERICA AND EARTH.
WITH THREE SECRET SERVICE AGENTS STANDING NEARBY, A FRIENDLY GERMAN SHEPHERD, TAIL WAGGING, JUMPS ONTO THE STAGE.
PLEASE JOIN US, MADAM PRESIDENT AND SPEAKER MATT. SO THAT YOU UNDERSTAND WHAT HAS INVADED EARTH, ALLOW ME TO INTRODUCE YOU TO SAMMY.
STAY, SAMMY.

A ROOM-SIZED CLEAR SHIELD RISES FROM THE FLOOR, ENCIRCLING SAMMY AS EVERYONE STEPS DOWN FROM THE STAGE.
OH! WE, TOO, ARE ANIMALS.
SAMMY IS ONE OF THE CREATURE'S VICTIMS AND HAS INFECTED SEVERAL OF US. LET'S WATCH ITS TRANSFORMATION AND IMAGINE HOW MANY PETS AND WILD ANIMALS ARE ON EARTH.
THE LOVABLE GERMAN SHEPHERD TRANSFORMS INTO A DOG-LIKE MONSTER THE SIZE OF A CLYDESDALE.
THE ENTIRE GROUP IS STARTLED AS THE CREATURE TURNS ITS HEAD TOWARDS PRESIDENT JAMES, STANDING BESIDE HARRIET TO THE RIGHT OF THE STAGE. THE THREE SECRET SERVICE AGENTS ARE A FEW FEET AWAY.

LUCY STONE TELEPATHICALLY REMINDS PRESIDENT JAMES TO STAY CALM.
STAY CALM. YOU ARE SAFE.
THREE SECRET SERVICE AGENTS RUSH TO PROTECT PRESIDENT JAMES STANDING NEAR SPEAKER MATT.
AGENT HICKS SHIELDS SPEAKER MATT AS TWO AGENTS SHIELD PRESIDENT JAMES.
CHIEF OF STAFF MARIA SANCHEZ IS FURIOUS AT AGENT HICKS' FAILURE TO PROTECT PRESIDENT JAMES.

THE BEAST FADES AWAY AS HARRIET WALKS TO THE CENTER OF THE STAGE.
THIS WAS A DEMONSTRATION. THE REALITY IS FAR WORSE. THIS IS A SMALL SAMPLE OF MICROV'S POWERS.
IT CAN DO MUCH MORE. YOUR GUNS WILL NOT HELP. THESE TOWERS ENSURE MICROV WILL NEVER ESCAPE EARTH. WE ARE HERE TO ENSURE IT NEVER DESTROYS HUMANITY.
HARRIET EXPRESSES SHE, TOO, IS IN AWE OF WHAT MR. D HAS CREATED.
AND THIS MR. D? WHAT IS HIS ROLE IN ALL THIS?
HE DESIGNED ALL THIS, IS IN CHARGE OF ALL THIS, AND IS THE BEING THE CREATURE FEARS MOST, AS IT SHOULD.
TRUTH POINTS TO A DOOR NEARBY.
THANK YOU, MADAM PRESIDENT. THAT DOOR WILL LEAD YOU THROUGH THE LOOKING GLASS AND BACK TO YOUR CONFERENCE ROOM.
PLEASE KNOW AS WE DO, AMERICA IS STRONGER BY YOUR SERVICE. WE ARE AVAILABLE TO YOU AND YOUR TEAM WHEN NEEDED.

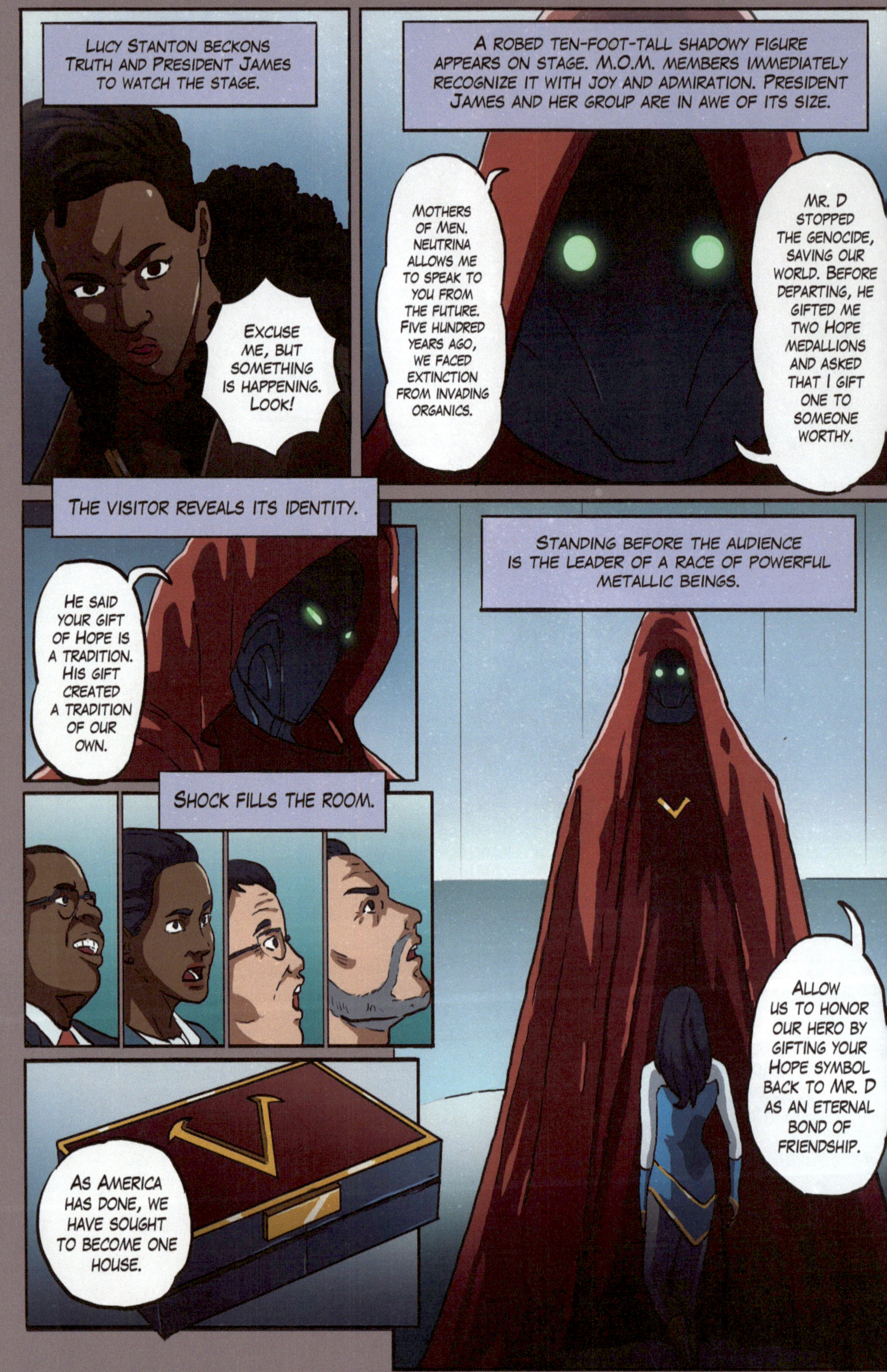

Lucy Stanton beckons Truth and President James to watch the stage.
A robed ten-foot-tall shadowy figure appears on stage. M.O.M. members immediately recognize it with joy and admiration. President James and her group are in awe of its size.
Excuse me, but something is happening. Look!
Mothers of Men. Neutrina allows me to speak to you from the future. Five hundred years ago, we faced extinction from invading organics.
Mr. D stopped the genocide, saving our world. Before departing, he gifted me two Hope Medallions and asked that I gift one to someone worthy.
The visitor reveals its identity.
He said your gift of Hope is a tradition. His gift created a tradition of our own.
Standing before the audience is the leader of a race of powerful metallic beings.
Shock fills the room.
Allow us to honor our hero by gifting your Hope symbol back to Mr. D as an eternal bond of friendship.
As America has done, we have sought to become one house.

MR. D AND NEUTRINA STAND ON A THIN PLATFORM EXTENDING 50 FEET FROM THE CHESAPEAKE BAY TOWER. POWERFUL LIGHTNING FLASHES INSIDE MASSIVE RAIN CLOUDS FAR BELOW AND RISING ABOVE THEM IN THE DISTANCE.
NEUTRINA FIRES A HIGH-ENERGY BLAST, STRIKING MR. D.
I AM HUMBLED BY THEIR GRATITUDE. THEIR LOVE EXTENDS TO YOU. TAKE ME HOME.
THEY DIVE TOWARDS THE CLOUDS BELOW WITH ARMS EXTENDED OUTWARD LIKE GLIDERS, SLOWLY CURVING AWAY FROM THE TOWER AND FLYING JUST ABOVE THE CLOUDS, ABSORBING ENERGY AS LIGHTNING BOLTS STRIKE THEM.

DAWN FEBRUARY 20, 1895, THE BACKYARD OF FREDERICK DOUGLASS'S HOME, CEDAR HILL. AN UNMASKED MR. D STANDS ALONE IN THE FAR END OF THE BACKYARD, LOOKING OUT AWAY FROM THE HOUSE. SEVENTY-SEVEN-YEAR-OLD FREDERICK DOUGLASS STANDS AT HIS BACK DOOR, WONDERING WHO HE IS.
FREDERICK DOUGLASS APPROACHES MR. D FROM BEHIND, WHO IS ENJOYING THE VIEW OF DISTANT TREES.
FD STUDIES MR. D'S FACE.
YOU LOOK FAMILIAR. HAVE WE MET?
CLOSE YOUR EYES, FREDERICK, AND BREATHE DEEPLY. I WILL DO THE SAME.
NOW, OPEN.
FREDERICK DOUGLASS OPENS HIS EYES TO FIND THEM STANDING ON A CLIFF ON THE EVIL SLAVE-BREAKER EDWARD COVEY'S FARM, WATCHING TALL SHIPS WITH TOWERING WHITE SAILS HEADING INTO THE HORIZON.
YES, AND I DID ESCAPE AND EVENTUALLY SAIL AWAY TO EUROPE LIKE THEM.
AS A SLAVE, IN YOUR YOUTH, YOU WOULD STAND HERE AND DREAM OF BEING FREE AND SAILING AWAY ON A SHIP LIKE THOSE.
YOU ARE ABOARD THE LEAD SHIP. TODAY, THEIR DESTINATION IS THE FUTURE, WHERE SOMEONE SPECIAL AWAITS YOUR ARRIVAL.
TONIGHT, YOU WILL MEND OLD WOUNDS, EVEN THOSE THAT HAVE CUT DEEP FOR YEARS.

FREDERICK DOUGLASS SEES KHALID STANDING NEAR THEM, WATCHING THE SHIPS SAILING AWAY.
WHO IS THE BOY? IS HE WITH YOU?
NO. HE IS WITH YOU. HE IS AMONG THE MILLIONS OF KIDS AND ADULTS YOUR LIFE HAS INSPIRED.
HE IS READING YOUR FIRST BOOK, NARRATIVE OF THE LIFE OF FREDERICK DOUGLASS, AN AMERICAN SLAVE.
THE CHESAPEAKE BAY VIEW IS BREATHTAKING.
HE IS DREAMING THE SAME DREAMS YOUR WRITINGS CREATED AND THE HOPE AND DETERMINATION YOU GAVE THEM.
THAT NIGHT, AFTER YEARS OF STRONG DISAGREEMENT ON VOTING RIGHTS FOR BLACK MEN FREDERICK DOUGLASS STANDS ON STAGE WITH 75-YEAR-OLD SUSAN B. ANTHONY AS THEY RECEIVE A STANDING OVATION FROM THE NATIONAL COUNCIL OF WOMEN
LATER THAT NIGHT, FREDERICK DOUGLASS PASSES AWAY SITTING IN A COMFORTABLE CHAIR IN HIS HOME.

FREDERICK DOUGLASS BECOMES THE FIRST TO JOIN HARRIET IN AMERICA 30,000 YEARS INTO THE FUTURE.

WHITE HOUSE OVAL OFFICE
SECRETARY OF DEFENSE DRAPER UPDATES PRESIDENT JAMES AND MARIA SANCHEZ ON THE AIR FORCE PILOTS SCRAMBLED TO THE COORDINATES OF THE FIRST TOWER TO APPEAR.
DR. DREW'S SUGGESTION TO REVIEW THE PILOTS' FLIGHT TIMES AND FUEL USE REVEALS STRANGE RESULTS.
THEY RETURNED TO BASE CARRYING TWICE THE ESTIMATED FUEL BASED ON FLIGHT TIMES. IMPOSSIBLE.
YOU JUST EXPERIENCED THE IMPOSSIBLE INSIDE A TOWER. WHY SHOULD IT BE ANY DIFFERENT OUTSIDE ONE?
EXCELLENT POINT, BUT WE ARE CONTINUING OUR INVESTIGATION, KNOWING THEY ARE WATCHING.
I'M SURE THEY WOULD EXPECT NOTHING LESS.
PRESIDENT JAMES ASKS BOTH THEIR IMPRESSIONS OF THE VISITORS FROM THE FUTURE.
OUR VISITORS, FRIEND OR FOE? GUT FEELING, NO HOLDING BACK.
FRIENDS
BIG TIME!
THANK GOODNESS!
PATRIOTS, HEROES; AND YOU, MADAM PRESIDENT, YOUR IMPRESSION?
A BAT BEAST FLOATS HIGH IN THE SKY, EMITTING SOUNDS THAT BOUNCE OFF THE STRUCTURES FAR BELOW, AND TRANSMITS THE DATA TO A HIBERNATING MicroV
I WAKE UP EVERY DAY PROUD TO BE AN AMERICAN. THEY ARE PROOF WE SHOULD ALL BE. I AM MORE DETERMINED THAN EVER TO BRING US CLOSER TO WHERE THEY ARE AS A PEOPLE.

LATE IN THE EVENING, AN ANGRY SPEAKER OF THE HOUSE, MATT, STANDS ALONE OUTSIDE THE UNITED STATES CAPITOL, ADMIRING ITS BEAUTY. HE SHOUTS UP AT THE CAPITOL.
SCREAMING!
HE MAKES A VOIP CALL.
THIS IS OUR HOUSE! OUR COUNTRY! THEY CAME TO PROTECT THEIR AMERICA FROM A MONSTER! WHO WILL PROTECT THEM FROM ME?!
CODE RED! THE CRISIS IS UPON US. SET A MEETING, ASPEN. HILLTOP HOUSE! IT'S DRAFT DAY! ONLY LOYAL HEARTLAND TEAM PLAYERS WHO THROW LONG, QUICK RELEASES AND SCRAMBLE FAST!

LATE NIGHT.
A RED-EYE JUMBO JET FROM WASHINGTON, D.C., TO LOS ANGELES
DR. DREW IS ONE OF THE FEW PASSENGERS AWAKE IN FIRST CLASS AS HE TALKS TO JOYCE.
HAVE AN IMAGE I HAVE TO PROTECT.
WE NEED TO KEEP THIS CONVERSATION SHORT, DEAR. THEY PUT ME IN FIRST CLASS. I NOW
DON'T YOU HANG UP THE PHONE?
I WAS IN A CONFERENCE ROOM BENEATH THE WHITE HOUSE. YOU WON'T BELIEVE WHERE I WAS AFTER EXITING THAT ROOM. WE NEED A MIND MELD. SPEAKING OF WHICH, HOW'S OUR MIND-MELDED DAUGHTER?
THAT'S BEAUTIFUL. LET'S MAKE IT A MONTHLY FAMILY AFFAIR AND GET OUR FRIENDS TO DONATE.
EXCUSE ME, DR. DREW.
HE LOOKS UP TO SEE NEUTRINA LOOKING DOWN AT HIM.

AS OTHERS SLEEP, NEUTRINA SUDDENLY APPEARS.
HELLO, DR. DREW. I AM NEUTRINA.
ONE MOMENT, PLEASE, WHILE I REMOVE MY MASK.
NEUTRINA APPEARS AS AFRICAN AMERICAN
THAT'S BETTER.
NEUTRINA NOW APPEARS AS ASIAN AMERICAN, MU. SHE ANSWERS USING HIS KIND OF HUMOR.
TELL ME AGAIN. WHO ARE YOU?
I AM ONE OF THE KLINGONS YOU'VE BEEN SEARCHING FOR.
NEUTRINA IS NOW NATIVE AMERICAN, TAU.
I AM AN ASTROPHYSICIST AND COSMOLOGIST. A LITTLE PROOF, PLEASE, BEFORE CONTINUING.
HE LOOKS AT NEUTRINA, EXPRESSIONLESS.
WHAT YOU'VE SEEN IS NOT ENOUGH? OK, PLEASE PRESS THE PALMS OF YOUR HANDS TOGETHER AS HARD AS YOU CAN UNTIL THEY MERGE.
NEUTRINO DOES THE SAME TO DR. DREW.

ARE WE ON TV? I CANNOT PERFORM THAT HAND TASK, AND NEITHER CAN YOU.
HOW ARE YOU CHANGING YOUR FACE? I THINK IT'S TIME I PRESS THE HELP BUTTON.
NOW WEARING HER MASK, NEUTRINA HOLDS HER PALMS FACING A FEW INCHES APART.
THIS CONVERSATION IS TAKING LESS THAN A SECOND. AND, NO, YOU ARE NOT ASLEEP. WATCH.
DR. DREW CONCEDES.
YOU HAVE MY UNDIVIDED ATTENTION.

MR.D REQUESTS A MEETING WITH YOU AND JOYCE REGARDING YOUR SON, KHALID. HE IS A GIFT YOU CAN GIVE TO THE UNIVERSE.
PLEASE DISCUSS OUR REQUEST WITH YOUR FAMILY, THEN LET US KNOW YOUR DECISION.
AND HOW DO WE DO THAT?

SIMPLE, SPEAK YOUR ANSWER. A GIFT WILL APPEAR AS PROOF OF THIS ENCOUNTER. THANK YOU FOR YOUR CONSIDERABLE TIME. THAT'S A JOKE. GOOD NIGHT.

DR. DREW TALKS TO HIMSELF.
CONSIDERABLE TIME. LESS THAN A SECOND.
NICE JOKE.

NIGHT
TWENTY ROWDY MOTORCYCLE CLUB MEMBERS ARE EN ROUTE TO THEIR FAVORITE BAR FOR DRINKS.
THEY NOTICE A STRANGE CAMP LIGHT IN THE DISTANT DESERT AND INVESTIGATE.
THE BIKERS APPROACH THE LIGHTS
THE BIKER GANG CAN'T BELIEVE WHAT THEY FIND.

STILL LOOKING UP AT THE STARS, HE SPEAKS. HE WAS ONCE ROBERT SMALLS. MR. D SENT HIM TO DELIVER A MESSAGE TO THE GANG LEADER.
YOU'RE LATE.
I'VE BEEN WAITING FOR HOURS. A WONDERFUL SURPRISE AWAITS YOU ON TITAN, ENCELADUS, AND JUPITER'S MOONS, ESPECIALLY EUROPA.
YOU WON'T LIKE MY SURPRISE. I WANT THAT BIKE. WHERE'D YOU PUT THE WHEELS?
I'M TALKING LIFE-CHANGING DISCOVERIES, AND YOU'RE TALKING BIKES?
THE BIKER PULLS HIS GUN AND FIRES SEVERAL SHOTS, KNOCKING ROBERT OFF HIS SKYCYCLE TO THE GROUND BEHIND IT.
THE LEADER IS FURIOUS THAT ONE OF HIS CREW SHOT A STRANGER WHO MEANT THEM NO HARM.
YOU DON'T NEED IT ANY MORE!
NO!
MEN DON'T KILL UNARMED MEN! YOU'RE OUT!
LOOK!
ROBERT IS STANDING BESIDE HIS SKYCYCLE, UNHARMED
I DIDN'T GET TO FINISH WHY I AM HERE WAITING FOR YOU. TEN YEARS AGO, ONE OF YOU FATHERED A SPECIAL GIRL.
YOU LOVED HER MOTHER WHO IS BLACK, BUT BROKE UP WITH HER BECAUSE OF PRESSURE FROM YOUR FAMILY, NOT KNOWING SHE WAS PREGNANT.
YOUR CHILD NEEDS YOU IN HER LIFE. FIND HER. SHE IS A UNIQUE GIFT TO THE UNIVERSE.

I WAS MARINE! I SHOT YOU, MAN! I DON'T MISS!
YES. YOU WERE A MARINE.
YOU SWORE AN OATH TO THE CONSTITUTION, RETURNED HOME, AND TRIED TO KILL SOMEONE WHO DID YOU NO HARM.
YOU ARE A DISGRACE TO THE CORPS.

BUT, TO ANSWER YOUR CONCERNS, YOU CANNOT SHOOT ME. I WON'T ALLOW IT.
ONE OF YOU HAS SOME SERIOUS DECISIONS TO MAKE. FOR TONIGHT, IF YOU WILL ALLOW, ALL DRINKS ON ME!
THEY HEAR ROARS IN THE DARKNESS SURROUNDING THEM

THE BIKERS ARE SURROUNDED BY SHADOWY MOVING IMAGE. VELOCIRAPTORS!
NO WORRY. FRIENDS OF MINE, IN CASE ANYONE TRIED TO LEAVE BEFORE I FINISHED WHAT I CAME HERE TO SAY. YOU'RE SAFE. THEY WON'T EAT YOU.

GRURAAAA!
GRURAAAA!
WHAT THE HELL IS THAT?

SUNSET
ASPEN / PITKIN COUNTY AIRPORT. MANY PRIVATE JETS ARE PARKED OFF THE RUNWAY AS MORE LAND. LIMOUSINES LINE UP TO MEET THEM. WE HEAR A VOICE IN THE A.T.C. TOWER.
SOMETHING BIG IS HAPPENING; MORE PRIVATE JETS THAN BIRDS. LOOK AT THE LIMOS AND SECURITY DETAILS! AND NO CAMERAS!
LATER - REMOTE ASPEN MANSION - AS A LARGE GROUP OF WEALTHY CONSPIRATORS ARE GATHERED IN A LARGE ROOM. SPEAKER MATT SPEAKS QUIETLY WITH TWO OLDER MEN.
GET BACK TO D.C. FINANCING? NO LIMITS.
OUR PLAN TO STEAL THE WHITE HOUSE IS AT RISK. THE PRESIDENT TREATS THEM LIKE FAMILY.
THEY COULD BE. I SAW WHAT THEY CAN DO. THEY ARE A THREAT! WE NEED TO ACT FAST!
WHATEVER YOU NEED, NO LIMITS.
WE'LL BE IN TOUCH. THE DRAFT IS GOING WELL.

I DO HAVE GOOD NEWS. THEY BROUGHT THEIR ARMY. THREE BEAUTIFUL WOMEN! I'M SHAKING IN MY BOOTS!
LOUD LAUGHTER!

SPEAKER MATT DRIVES ALONE IN A CAR DOWN
A REMOTE MOUNTAIN ROAD TOWARD THE DISTANT CITY LIGHTS.

INSIDE, SPEAKER MATT
IS UNCONSCIOUS.

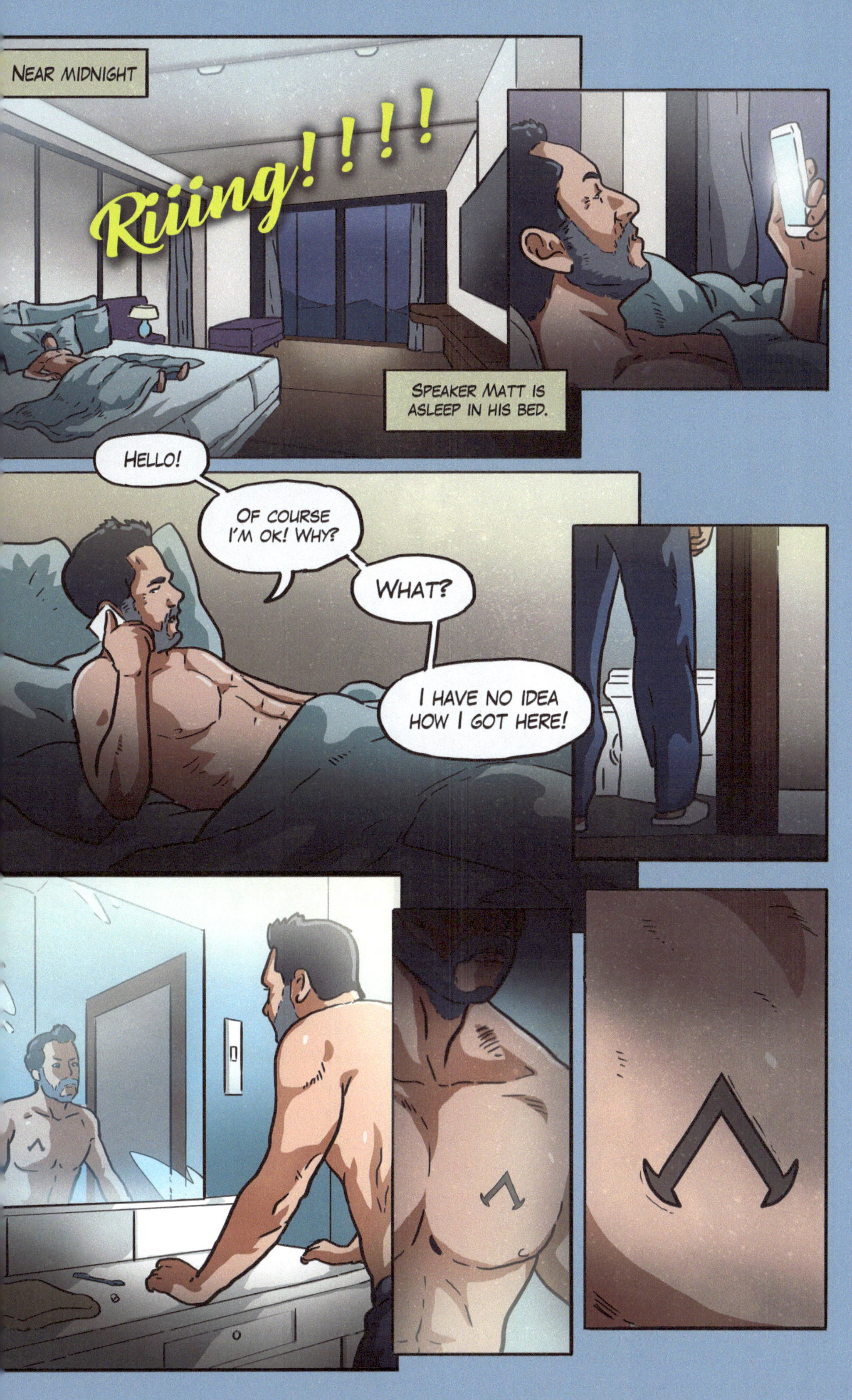

NEAR MIDNIGHT
Riiing!!!!
SPEAKER MATT IS ASLEEP IN HIS BED.
HELLO!
OF COURSE I'M OK! WHY?
WHAT?
I HAVE NO IDEA HOW I GOT HERE!

SIX A.M. THE NEXT DAY
MONTGOMERY, ALABAMA.
VIKKI HOPE, A SENIOR ATTORNEY FOR THE EQUAL JUSTICE INITIATIVE TEAM, WALKS ACROSS THE NATIONAL MEMORIAL FOR PEACE AND JUSTICE GROUNDS. SHE APPROACHES TWO WOMEN ALREADY THERE ADMIRING THE EXHIBITS. THEY ARE M.O.M. MEMBERS IDA BELL WELLS AND JESSIE DANIEL AMES. BOTH CHAMPIONED ANTI-LYNCHING CAUSES DURING THE LATE 1800s AND EARLY 1900s.
HELLO. THANK YOU FOR YOUR INTEREST, BUT WE ARE NOT OPEN YET.
AND I AM JESSIE. IT IS TRULY AN HONOR TO MEET YOU.
HELLO VIKKI, WE ARE HERE TO SEE YOU. I AM IDA.
VIKKI IS SURPRISED THEY KNOW HER BUT DON'T REALIZE WHO THEY ARE.
IDA AND JESSIE ARE TWO OF MY FAVORITE NAMES. HOW CAN I HELP YOU?
AH! YOU'VE DONE YOUR HOMEWORK. WE USE CORTEN STEEL TO MAKE OUR MONUMENTS. IT IS VERY STRONG AND CAN WITHSTAND THE ELEMENTS.
SHE WAS DESCRIBING YOU, NOT THE MONUMENTS. WE ARE FANS. YOUR TEAM AT EJI AND OTHERS LIKE YOU ACROSS AMERICA ARE SLOWLY MOVING THIS GREAT NATION CLOSER TO THAT "PERFECT UNION."
CORTEN STEEL.
THE ENTIRE M.O.M. GROUP IS WAITING TO GREET HER BESIDE A SMALL STAGE WHERE A BLANK MONUMENT STANDS ALONE.
THANK YOU. WE ARE A COMMUNITY, NOT ONE. WHY ARE YOU HERE?
TO COLLECT A MONUMENT. WE HAVE BEEN AWAITING YOUR ARRIVAL. PLEASE WALK INSIDE WITH US.

HARRIET GREETS VIKKI WHILE OTHERS APPLAUD.
HELLO, VIKKI. WE ARE FRIENDS. WE APOLOGIZE FOR STARTING YOUR DAY LIKE THIS.
HOWEVER, WE HAVE COME A LONG WAY TO COLLECT OUR MONUMENT.
BUT YOU HAVE CHOSEN A BLANK. WHY?
HARRIET POINTS TO THE ENTRANCE OF THE CHAMBER.
LOOK.
TAKE MY HAND AND WATCH. THIS MOMENT IS FOR THOSE WHO SHARE YOUR DEDICATION TO EQUAL JUSTICE. THEY WILL FEEL THIS.
YOU WILL SOON KNOW.
EVERYONE APPLAUDS AS THEY WATCH THE RESULTS OF THE BLASTS. VIKKI SMILES.
BEAUTIFUL! THIS IS WHAT WE FIGHT FOR EVERY DAY! BUT WHERE WILL YOU TAKE IT?
MR. D AND NEUTRINA FIRE ENERGY BLASTS AT THE MONUMENT.

WHAT NEXT?
I'M ALREADY SPEECHLESS.
WAIT! IDA AND JESSIE?
VIKKI LOOKS AT IDA AND JESSIE.
WHAT ARE YOUR FULL NAMES?
JESSIE DANIELS AMES.
IDA BELL WELLS.
SHOCK!
MY GOODNESS!
HARRIET GIVES VIKKI A JEWELRY BOX CONTAINING A HOPE MEDALLION.
VIKKI, YOU AND THE THOUSANDS WHO TIRELESSLY SERVE THOSE WITHOUT HOPE, WON.
I HAD THE SAME REACTION WHEN I FIRST MET THEM.
PLEASE ACCEPT THIS GIFT FOR YOUR PAST AND FUTURE VICTORIES, PUSHING US TO THAT "MORE PERFECT UNION."
LEAVE IT ON YOUR DESK TONIGHT. TOMORROW, GIVE ONE TO EACH TEAM MEMBER. THE FUTURE AWAITS YOUR ARRIVAL.

THE SAME MORNING, IN THE CENTER OF THE U.S. CAPITOL ROTUNDA, PROTECTED BY GOLD STANCHIONS WITH RED VELVET ROPES, FLOATS THE MONUMENT.

ONE ENGRAVED WIDE SIDE FACES THE SENATE, AND THE OTHER FACES THE HOUSE OF REPRESENTATIVES. BOTH SAY THE SAME.
BEAUTIFUL WORDS.
SO TRUE.
IF ONLY WE GOVERNED WITH THIS IN MIND!
A MESSAGE TO CONGRESS IS ENGRAVED ON EACH SIDE, ONE WORD PER LINE: "EQUAL VALUE FOR EVERY LIFE."
EQUAL
VALUE
FOR
EVERY
LIFE

SAME DAY – NEW SITUATION ROOM UNDER WHITE HOUSE – HARRIET, TRUTH, AND THE LUCYS MEET WITH PRESIDENT JAMES, VP BILL TRAVIS, AND DEFENSE SECRETARY DRAPER. MILITARY HEADS AND SENIOR OFFICIALS APPEAR ON WALL MONITORS.
VP BILL TRAVIS
THANK YOU FOR COMING. MY TEAM HAS QUESTIONS REGARDING THE TOWERS.
PLEASE ASK.
HELLO. I'M HONORED TO MEET YOU. TOWERS TO THE HEAVENS! APPEAR IN SECONDS! IMPRESSIVE, BUT IMPOSSIBLE! HOW?
THOUSANDS OF LIVES COULD BE LOST IF ONE IS SABOTAGED AND FALLS.
THE MISSILES WOULD RUN OUT OF FUEL. TERRORISTS CANNOT DEFEAT SPACETIME.
YOU CAN ONLY TOUCH A TOWER IF IT WANTS TO BE TOUCHED.
FEEL FREE TO TRY BY WHATEVER MEANS YOU LIKE. YOU HAVE OUR PERMISSION.
THESE ARE OUR PORTABLE UNITS, OUR SMALLEST.
CLARIFY, PLEASE. WHAT IF WE FIRED CRUISE MISSILES OR TERRORISTS SENT TEAMS TO BLOW ONE UP?
THE SPACE OPERATIONS DIRECTOR SPEAKS FROM A SCREEN.
WHAT ARE THEY? CAN MY TEAM INSPECT ONE?
YES, YOUR TEAM CAN INSPECT ONE WITH THE PRESIDENT'S APPROVAL.
AS COMMANDER IN CHIEF, SHE HAS TOTAL ACCESS. OH! NOTICED A CHANGE IN AIR QUALITY?
WHAT POWERS THE TOWERS?
CORRECT, MADAM PRESIDENT!
THEY ARE AI SPACETIME LIFEFORMS DESIGNED BY MR. D. THEIR DIRECTIVE IS TO PROTECT AND PRESERVE.
LET ME GUESS, OUR SUN AND THE EARTH'S CORE.

DO NOT BELIEVE THE LIES THESE INVADERS TELL.
THEY ARE HERE TO TAKE OUR COUNTRY AND DESTROY OUR WAY OF LIFE.
PRESENT - SPEAKER MATT SPEAKS TO A LARGE GATHERING FROM A LARGE SCREEN IN A LIBRARY INSIDE AN OLD MANSION.
WE HAVE AN ANSWER TO THEIR PLANS: CRUSH THEM FIRST!
TEAMS ARE DEPLOYING TO ALL TOWER LOCATIONS, PREPARED TO DIE FOR THEIR COUNTRY. THE INVADERS WILL NOT KNOW WHAT HIT THEM.
BEFORE YOU DEPLOY, SEND ME THE CAMP COORDINATES. MY TEAM WILL MEET WITH THEM TONIGHT FOR LAST-MINUTE MOTIVATION. THEY WILL BE UNSTOPPABLE.
LATE NIGHT - SCREAMS FILL THE AIR IN REMOTE WOODS AS THOUSANDS OF BATS SWARM IN REMOTE CAMP CABINS INSIDE AND OUT WHILE ONE MASSIVE BAT-LIKE CREATURE WATCHES FROM THE DARKNESS.
AAAAAA
AHHHH

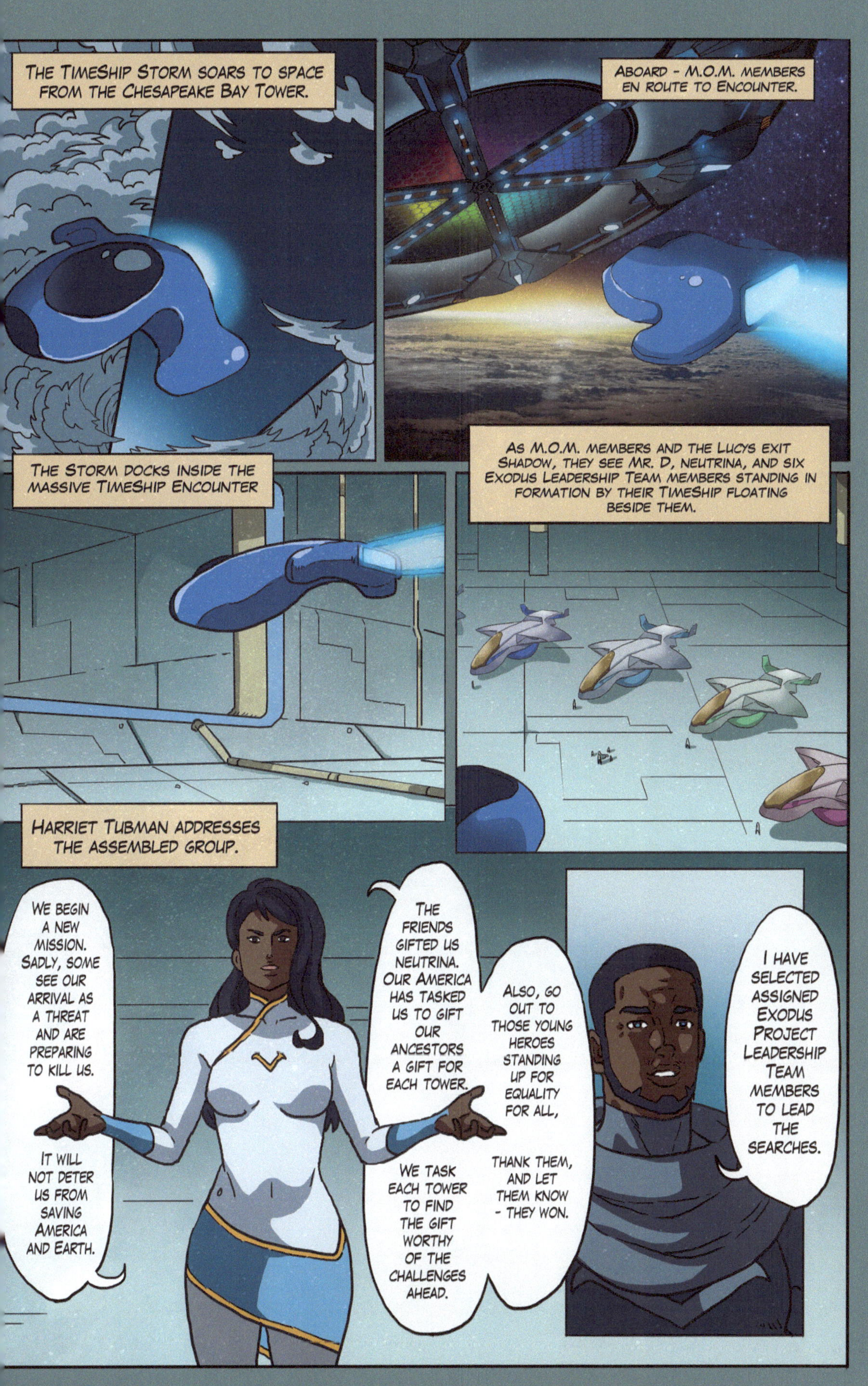

THE TIMESHIP STORM SOARS TO SPACE FROM THE CHESAPEAKE BAY TOWER.
ABOARD - M.O.M. MEMBERS EN ROUTE TO ENCOUNTER.
THE STORM DOCKS INSIDE THE MASSIVE TIMESHIP ENCOUNTER
AS M.O.M. MEMBERS AND THE LUCYS EXIT SHADOW, THEY SEE MR. D, NEUTRINA, AND SIX EXODUS LEADERSHIP TEAM MEMBERS STANDING IN FORMATION BY THEIR TIMESHIP FLOATING BESIDE THEM.
HARRIET TUBMAN ADDRESSES THE ASSEMBLED GROUP.
WE BEGIN A NEW MISSION. SADLY, SOME SEE OUR ARRIVAL AS A THREAT AND ARE PREPARING TO KILL US.
IT WILL NOT DETER US FROM SAVING AMERICA AND EARTH.
THE FRIENDS GIFTED US NEUTRINA. OUR AMERICA HAS TASKED US TO GIFT OUR ANCESTORS A GIFT FOR EACH TOWER.
WE TASK EACH TOWER TO FIND THE GIFT WORTHY OF THE CHALLENGES AHEAD.
ALSO, GO OUT TO THOSE YOUNG HEROES STANDING UP FOR EQUALITY FOR ALL,
THANK THEM, AND LET THEM KNOW - THEY WON.
I HAVE SELECTED ASSIGNED EXODUS PROJECT LEADERSHIP TEAM MEMBERS TO LEAD THE SEARCHES.

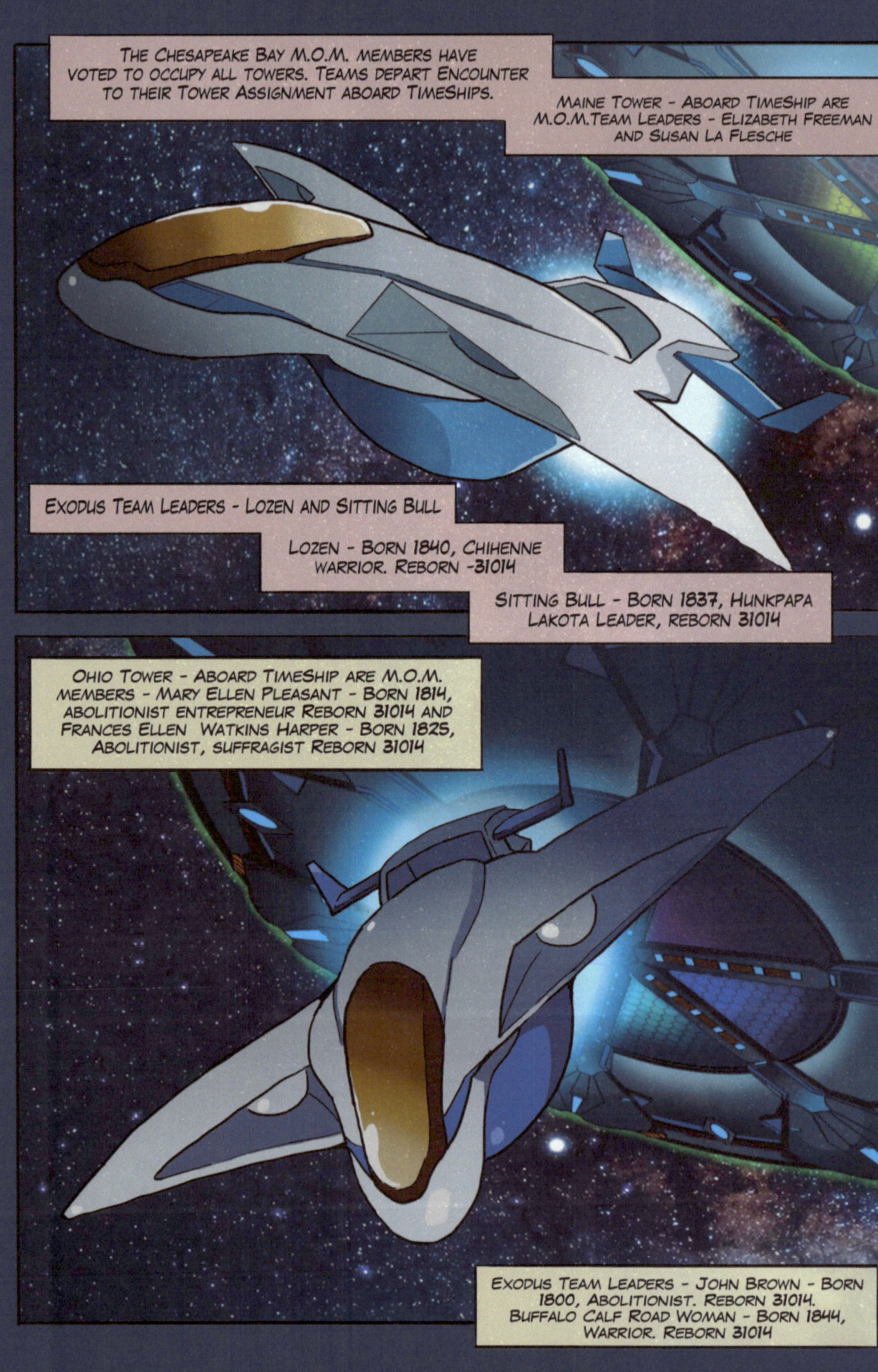

THE CHESAPEAKE BAY M.O.M. MEMBERS HAVE VOTED TO OCCUPY ALL TOWERS. TEAMS DEPART ENCOUNTER TO THEIR TOWER ASSIGNMENT ABOARD TIMESHIPS.
MAINE TOWER - ABOARD TIMESHIP ARE M.O.M. TEAM LEADERS - ELIZABETH FREEMAN AND SUSAN LA FLESCHE
EXODUS TEAM LEADERS - LOZEN AND SITTING BULL
LOZEN - BORN 1840, CHIHENNE WARRIOR. REBORN -31014
SITTING BULL - BORN 1837, HUNKPAPA LAKOTA LEADER, REBORN 31014
OHIO TOWER - ABOARD TIMESHIP ARE M.O.M. MEMBERS - MARY ELLEN PLEASANT - BORN 1814, ABOLITIONIST ENTREPRENEUR REBORN 31014 AND FRANCES ELLEN WATKINS HARPER - BORN 1825, ABOLITIONIST, SUFFRAGIST REBORN 31014
EXODUS TEAM LEADERS - JOHN BROWN - BORN 1800, ABOLITIONIST. REBORN 31014. BUFFALO CALF ROAD WOMAN - BORN 1844, WARRIOR. REBORN 31014

THE GULF OF MEXICO TOWER - ABOARD TIMESHIP ARE M.O.M. - MARY ANN SHADD CARY BORN 1823, SLAVERY ACTIVIST, REBORN 31014 SARAH MAPP DOUGLASS BORN 1806 ABOLITIONIST, REBORN 31014
EXODUS TEAM LEADERS - WONG CHIN FOO BORN 1847 REBORN 31014 ADOLFO FERNÁNDEZ CAVADA BORN 1832 UNION OFFICER REBORN 31014
MISSOURI TOWER - ABOARD TIMESHIP ARE M.O.M. MEMBERS - MARIA W. STEWART - BORN 1803 ABOLITIONIST REBORN 31014 SARAH WINNEMUCCA - NORTHERN PAIUTE WRITER, ACTIVIST REBORN 31014
EXODUS TEAM LEADERS - WILLIAM LLOYD GARRISON BORN 1805 ABOLITIONIST, REBORN 31014 PRETTY NOSE BORN 1851, ARAPAHO WARRIOR, REBORN 31014

THE COAST OF NORTH CAROLINA TOWER - ABOARD TIMESHIP ARE M.O.M. - C. J. WALKER - BORN 1867, ENTREPRENEUR, POLITICAL AND SOCIAL ACTIVIST REBORN 31014 PINE LEAF, BORN 1806, BIAWACHEEITCHISH CHIEF AND WARRIOR, REBORN 31014
EXODUS TEAM LEADERS - WILLIAM STILL BORN 1819 ABOLITIONIST, UNDERGROUND RAILROAD FATHER, REBORN 31014 NAT TURNER, BORN 1800, LED THE SLAVE REBELLION, REBORN 31014 DAVID WALKER, BORN 1796, ABOLITIONIST, REBORN 31014
THE COAST OF NEW YORK TOWER - ABOARD TIMESHIP ARE M.O.M. - LUCRETIA MOTT, IDA BELL WELLS-BARNETT, AND SUSAN B. ANTHONY
EXODUS TEAM LEADERS - JAMES FORTEN, BORN 1766, ABOLITIONIST, REBORN 31014 ROBERT SMALLS, BORN 1839, POLITICIAN, REBORN 31014 JUANA RAMIREZ, BORN 1813, AFRO-VENEZUELAN COMMANDER 100-STRONG ALL-FEMALE ARTILLERY UNIT, REBORN 31014.
THE CHESAPEAKE BAY TOWER - ABOARD THE STORM IS M.O.M. - HARRIET TUBMAN, SOJOURNER TRUTH
EXODUS TEAM LEADERS - JOHN BINGHAM, BORN 1815, POLITICIAN AND ABOLITIONIST, REBORN 31014 CHARLES SUMNER, BORN 1811, POLITICIAN AND ABOLITIONIST, REBORN 31014 THADDEUS STEVENS, BORN 1792, POLITICIAN AND ABOLITIONIST, REBORN 31014 DON PIO DE JESUS PICO IV, BORN 1801, CALIFORNIA POLITICIAN, REBORN 31014
THEIR HOSTS - THE THREE LUCYS
DAVID RUGGLES BORN 1810 ABOLITIONIST, REBORN 31013

DOCTORS MANNY AND JOYCE DREW HOME DINING ROOM. MANNY SHARES ABOUT THE STRANGE MEETING HE HAD ON HIS FLIGHT HOME.

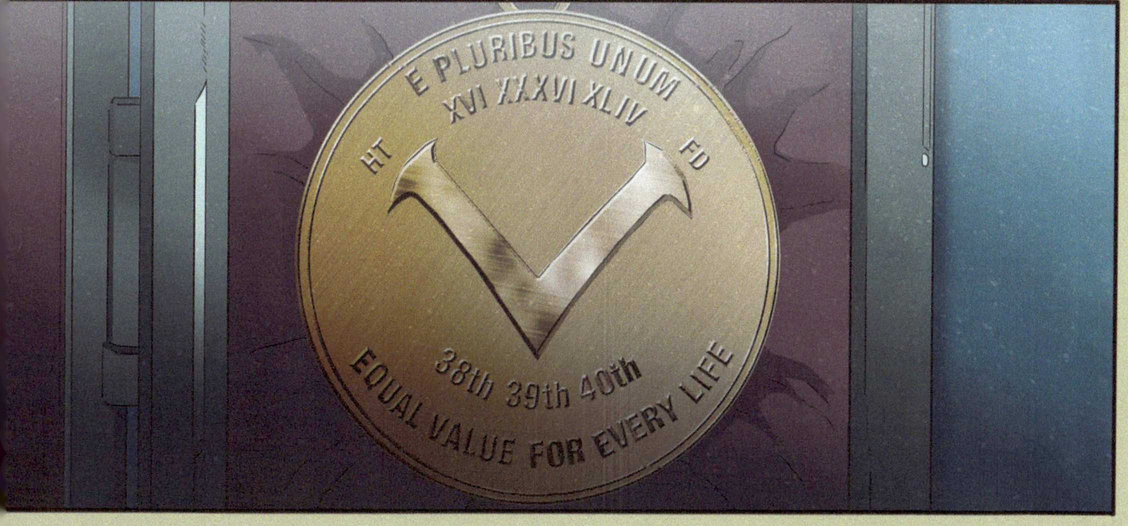

HARRIET, TRUTH, MR. D, AND NEUTRINA WATCH THE WHITE HOUSE ON A LARGE SCREEN INSIDE THE CHESAPEAKE BAY TOWER.
IT STARTS AGAIN.
THIS WORLD IS MINE.
TO BE CONTINUED...

EARTH ENCOUNTERS

THE ARRIVAL

THE SEVEN TOWERS

By neutrina

TOWER DESIGNER / AMBASSADOR

Frederick Douglass

Frederick Douglass (1818-1895) was a seminal African American social reformer, orator, writer, and statesman. Born into slavery in Maryland, he escaped to freedom and became a leading abolitionist. Douglass's powerful speeches and writings, including his autobiography "Narrative of the Life of Frederick Douglass, an American Slave," galvanized the anti-slavery movement. He also championed women's rights and advocated for equality and justice. Douglass's legacy as a tireless crusader against slavery and for human rights continues to inspire movements for social justice globally.

Maine Tower

M.O.M. TEAM LEADERS

Elizabeth Freeman (Mumbet)

Mumbet, later known as Elizabeth Freeman (1744-1829), was a pioneering African American woman whose legal battle helped end slavery in Massachusetts. Born into slavery in Claverack, New York, Mumbet endured years of harsh treatment. Inspired by the ideals of freedom and equality expressed in the Massachusetts Constitution, she sought legal counsel to challenge her enslavement. In 1781, represented by attorney Theodore Sedgwick, Mumbet won her case in Brom and Bett v. Ashley, leading to her emancipation. This landmark decision set a precedent for the abolition of slavery in Massachusetts. After gaining her freedom, Mumbet worked for the Sedgwick family and became a respected healer and midwife. Her courageous fight for liberty and justice remains a powerful testament to the enduring human spirit and the pursuit of equality.

Susan La Flesche Picotte

Susan La Flesche Picotte (1865-1915) was a trailblazing Native American physician
and social reformer. Born on the Omaha Reservation in Nebraska, she was
the first Native American woman to earn a medical degree in the United
States, graduating from the Woman's Medical College of Pennsylvania in 1889.
Dr. La Flesche Picotte dedicated her life to providing healthcare to the Omaha
people, often traveling long distances to treat patients in remote areas. Beyond
her medical practice, she advocated for public health, sanitation, and temperance,
working tirelessly to improve living conditions on the reservation. She also played
a crucial role in educating her community about health and wellness. Her pioneering
achievements and unwavering commitment to her people have left a lasting legacy
in the medical field and Native American history, exemplifying resilience,
compassion, and dedication to social justice.

ENCOUNTER EXODUS TEAM LEADERS

Lozen

Lozen (1840-1889) was a fearless Apache warrior and prophetess. Sister to the famed
Chief Victorio, she played a crucial role in the Apache resistance against Mexican and
American forces. Renowned for her strategic acumen and spiritual insights, Lozen
was often called upon to lead warriors in battle. Her bravery and dedication to her
people's freedom and survival made her a legendary figure in Apache history.
Lozen's legacy as a warrior and protector endures as a symbol of strength and resilience.

Sitting Bull

Sitting Bull (1831-1890) was a renowned Hunkpapa Lakota Sioux leader and spiritual
figure. Born in South Dakota, he rose to prominence for his unyielding resistance
against U.S. government policies that encroached on Native American lands. Sitting
Bull is best known for his leadership during the Battle of the Little Bighorn in 1876,
where his vision and strategy led to a decisive victory against General Custer's forces.
A symbol of Native American resistance, he joined Buffalo Bill's Wild West Show, using
the platform to advocate for his people's rights. Sitting Bull's legacy endures as
a powerful emblem of resistance, sovereignty, and the enduring spirit of Native
American culture.

Ohio Tower

M.O.M. TEAM LEADERS

Frances Ellen Watkins Harper

Frances Ellen Watkins Harper (1825-1911) was a prominent African American poet, author, and social reformer. Born free in Baltimore, Maryland, she became a leading voice in the abolitionist movement, using her writings and lectures to advocate for the end of slavery and civil rights. Harper published several poetry collections, novels, and essays, including "Poems on Miscellaneous Subjects" and "Iola Leroy." She also participated actively in the women's suffrage movement, co-founding the National Association of Colored Women. Harper's powerful words and tireless activism significantly advanced the causes of abolition, women's rights, and racial equality.

Mary Ellen Pleasant

Mary Ellen Pleasant (1814-1904) was a trailblazing entrepreneur, abolitionist, and philanthropist. Born into slavery in Georgia, she later moved to San Francisco, where she amassed significant wealth through savvy investments. Pleasant used her resources to support the Underground Railroad, aiding fugitive slaves. Known as the "Mother of Civil Rights in California," she tirelessly fought against racial discrimination and for the rights of African Americans. Her legacy as a fearless advocate and benefactor remains a testament to her enduring impact on social justice.

ENCOUNTER EXODUS TEAM LEADERS

John Brown

John Brown (1800-1859) was a radical American abolitionist whose fervent opposition to slavery led to his involvement in violent actions aimed at ending the institution. Born in Connecticut, Brown believed in direct action against slavery, culminating in his 1859 raid on the federal armory at Harpers Ferry. Although the raid failed and Brown was captured and executed, his bold stand against slavery galvanized the abolitionist movement and heightened tensions leading up to the Civil War. Brown's legacy as a martyr for justice and a catalyst for change continues to resonate in the struggle for civil rights.

Buffalo Calf Road Woman

Buffalo Calf Road Woman (c. 1844-1879) was a courageous Northern Cheyenne warrior known for her pivotal role in the Battle of the Rosebud and the Battle of the Little Bighorn. Born in present-day Montana, she gained legendary status when she saved her brother in the Battle of the Rosebud, which boosted her people's morale. At the Battle of the Little Bighorn, her participation was crucial in the defeat of Custer's forces. Her bravery and leadership exemplify the strength and resilience of Native American women, cementing her legacy as a heroic figure in Cheyenne history.

Gulf of Mexico Tower

M.O.M. TEAM LEADERS

Mary Ann Shadd Cary

Mary Ann Shadd Cary (1823-1893) was a trailblazing African American educator, journalist, and lawyer. Born free in Delaware, she became the first Black woman in North America to publish the Provincial Freeman newspaper, advocating for abolition and women's rights. Shadd Cary also played a crucial role in the Underground Railroad, helping escaped enslaved people find freedom in Canada. Later, she earned a law degree, becoming one of the first Black female lawyers in the United States. Her relentless pursuit of justice and equality and her pioneering contributions to journalism and law cement her legacy as a formidable advocate for civil rights.

Sarah Mapp Douglass

Sarah Mapp Douglass (1806-1882) was an influential African American educator, abolitionist, and women's rights advocate. Born into a prominent Philadelphia family, she dedicated her life to education and social reform. Douglass founded a school for black children, emphasizing science and moral philosophy. An active member of the Philadelphia Female Anti-Slavery Society, she collaborated with prominent abolitionists and used her writing to challenge racial and gender inequalities. Her work as an educator and reformer impacted the African American community, advancing educational opportunities and social justice.

ENCOUNTER EXODUS TEAM LEADERS

Wong Chin Foo

Wong Chin Foo (1847-1898) was a pioneering Chinese-American journalist and civil rights activist. Born in China, he immigrated to the United States and became a leading voice against anti-Chinese sentiment. Wong founded the first Chinese-language newspaper in the U.S. and challenged discriminatory laws, promoting understanding between Chinese and American communities. His advocacy for Chinese American rights and contributions to journalism and community organizing helped lay the groundwork for future generations in the fight for racial equality and immigrant rights.

Adolfo Fernandez Cavada

Adolfo Fernández Cavada (1832-1871) was a distinguished Cuban-American soldier, diplomat, and revolutionary leader. Born in Cuba and raised in Philadelphia, he served as a captain in the Union Army during the American Civil War, where his skill in creating detailed battlefield maps proved invaluable. After the war, Cavada returned to Cuba to support the fight for independence from Spain. He demonstrated exceptional leadership and bravery as a general in the Ten Years' War. Cavada was also appointed as the Cuban representative to the United States, advocating for Cuban independence on the international stage. Captured and executed by Spanish forces in 1871, his martyrdom galvanized the Cuban independence movement. Adolfo Fernández Cavada's legacy is celebrated for his unwavering dedication to the causes of freedom and justice in both the United States and Cuba.

Missouri Tower

M.O.M. TEAM LEADERS

Maria W. Stewart

Maria W. Stewart (1803-1879) was a pioneering African American orator, writer, and women's rights activist. Born free in Connecticut, Stewart became one of the first American women to speak publicly on political issues, addressing both racial and gender equality. Her bold speeches and writings in the 1830s called for abolition and women's education, challenging her time's deeply entrenched social norms. Stewart's pioneering voice and unwavering commitment to justice and equality have inspired generations of activists, marking her as a significant figure in the early fight for civil rights and women's suffrage.

Sarah Winnemucca

Sarah Winnemucca (1844-1891) was a pioneering Northern Paiute author, educator, and activist. Born in present-day Nevada, she was a granddaughter of the Paiute Chief Truckee. Fluent in English, Spanish, and several Native American languages, Winnemucca became a crucial liaison between her people and the U.S. government. She tirelessly advocated for Native American rights, exposing injustices and fighting for her people's survival through lectures and writings. Her autobiography, *Life Among the Piutes: Their Wrongs and Claims* (1883), is one of the first known works by a Native American woman and provides a vivid account of her people's struggles.
Winnemucca also established a school for Native American children, emphasizing cultural preservation and education. Her legacy as a passionate advocate for justice and equality endures, symbolizing the resilience and strength of her people.

ENCOUNTER EXODUS TEAM LEADERS

William Lloyd Garrison

William Lloyd Garrison (1805-1879) was a fervent American abolitionist,
journalist, and social reformer. Born in Massachusetts, he founded
the influential anti-slavery newspaper, *The Liberator*, in 1831, which became
a powerful voice for the abolitionist movement. Garrison's uncompromising
stance on immediate emancipation and his advocacy for equal rights made
him a central figure in the fight against slavery. He also co-founded
the American Anti-Slavery Society, rallying thousands to the cause. Garrison's
relentless pursuit of justice and his eloquent writings significantly advanced
the abolitionist movement, cementing his legacy as a pivotal champion
of human rights and equality.

Pretty Nose

Pretty Nose (c. 1851-1952) was a distinguished Arapaho warrior and respected
elder. She played a crucial role in the Battle of the Little Bighorn in 1876, fighting
alongside her people against General Custer's forces. Known for her bravery
and leadership, Pretty Nose symbolized strength and resilience. Living to
the age of 101, she witnessed immense changes in her lifetime and served
as a living bridge between generations. Her legacy as a warrior and a respected
figure in her community endures, embodying the Arapaho people's enduring
spirit and cultural heritage.

North Carolina Tower

M.O.M. TEAM LEADERS

Pine Leaf

**Pine Leaf (c. 1806-1854), also known as Woman Chief, was a legendary
warrior and leader of the Crow Nation. Captured and adopted by the Crow
as a child, she quickly rose to prominence due to her exceptional skills in combat
and leadership. Pine Leaf earned the title of "Bíawacheeitchish," meaning "
Woman Chief," after demonstrating unparalleled bravery in battle.
She led war parties and defended her people with fierce determination.
Pine Leaf's remarkable life defied gender norms and showcased the strength
and leadership of Native American women, leaving a lasting legacy
in the history of the Crow Nation.

Madam C. J. Walker

Madam C.J. Walker, born Sarah Breedlove, was a trailblazer in the beauty industry and a beacon of African American success. Born on December 23, 1867, in Delta, Louisiana, Walker overcame the constraints of poverty and the legacy of slavery to become the first female self-made millionaire in America. Her innovative hair care products and the "Walker System" revolutionized black hair care, empowering African American women with both beauty solutions and economic opportunities. Walker's entrepreneurial spirit was matched by her philanthropy; she supported the NAACP, the Black YMCA, and other causes. Her estate, Villa Lewaro, was a cultural salon for the Harlem Renaissance, symbolizing her unprecedented achievements as a businesswoman and activist. Walker's legacy endures, inspiring generations with her life's motto: "I got my start by giving myself a start!"1.

ENCOUNTER EXODUS TEAM LEADERS

William Still

William Still (1821-1902) was a prominent African American abolitionist, writer, and conductor on the Underground Railroad.
Born to formerly enslaved parents in New Jersey, Still assisted hundreds of fugitive slaves to freedom, meticulously documenting their stories.
His seminal work, "The Underground Railroad Records," provides invaluable historical insights into the struggles and triumphs of those escaping bondage. Still's dedication to abolition and his role in preserving these crucial narratives underscore his lasting impact on American history and the fight for freedom.

Nat Turner

Nat Turner (1800-1831) was an enslaved African American preacher who led a significant slave rebellion in Virginia in 1831. Deeply religious, Turner believed he was divinely chosen to lead his people to freedom. His uprising resulted in the deaths of approximately 60 white people and prompted severe reprisals, leading to the execution of Turner and many others. Turner's rebellion intensified the national debate over slavery, contributing to the growing abolitionist movement. His legacy is a complex symbol of resistance and the relentless pursuit of freedom.

David Walker

David Walker (1796-1830) was an African American abolitionist and writer whose radical pamphlet, "Appeal to the Coloured Citizens of the World," published in 1829, called for the immediate abolition of slavery and equal rights for Black people. Born free in North Carolina, Walker's powerful and provocative writings condemned the brutality of slavery and urged enslaved people to rise against their oppressors. His work significantly influenced the abolitionist movement and remains a seminal text in the history of African American resistance.

M.O.M. TEAM LEADERS

Lucretia Mott

Lucretia Mott (1793-1880) was a pioneering American Quaker, abolitionist, women's rights activist, and social reformer. Born in Nantucket, Massachusetts, the Quaker belief in equality and justice profoundly influenced her.
Mott became a fervent advocate for the abolition of slavery, co-founding the Philadelphia Female Anti-Slavery Society in 1833.
Her eloquent speeches and unwavering commitment drew national attention. Mott's activism extended to women's rights, and she played a crucial role in organizing the Seneca Falls Convention in 1848, which marked the beginning of the women's suffrage movement in the United States.
Her relentless pursuit of social justice, grounded in her deep moral convictions, left an indelible mark on American history, inspiring future generations to continue the fight for equality and human rights.

Susan B. Anthony

Susan B. Anthony (1820-1906) was a trailblazing American social reformer and women's rights activist whose tireless efforts helped secure women's suffrage in the United States. Born in Adams, Massachusetts, Anthony was raised in a Quaker family committed to social equality. She became a key figure in the women's suffrage movement, co-founding the National Woman Suffrage Association in 1869 with Elizabeth Cady Stanton. Anthony's dedication to the cause was unwavering; she organized, lectured, and campaigned nationwide, often facing arrest and public scorn. In 1872, she was famously arrested for voting illegally, a bold act of civil disobedience that underscored her commitment to equality. Her relentless advocacy laid the groundwork for the eventual passage of the 19th Amendment in 1920, which granted women the right to vote. Anthony's legacy as a champion of women's rights and social justice continues to inspire generations of activists.

Ida Bell Wells Barnett

**Ida B. Wells-Barnett (1862-1931) was a pioneering African American journalist, educator, and civil rights activist. Born into slavery in Mississippi, she dedicated her life to fighting racial injustice and violence. Wells gained national prominence with her investigative journalism, documenting lynchings and exposing their brutal reality. She co-founded the NAACP and worked tirelessly for women's suffrage, emphasizing the intersectionality of race and gender. Her courage in confronting systemic racism and advocating for justice left an indelible mark on American history, inspiring future generations of activists.

ENCOUNTER EXODUS TEAM LEADERS

James Forten

James Forten (1766-1842) was a prominent African American abolitionist, businessman, and philanthropist. Born free in Philadelphia, he became a successful sailmaker and used his wealth to support the abolitionist cause. Forten was an active member of the Pennsylvania Abolition Society and worked tirelessly to end slavery and promote civil rights for African Americans. His influential advocacy and generous financial support for anti-slavery initiatives significantly advanced the fight for freedom and equality, impacting American history.

Juana Ramírez

Juana Ramírez (1790-1856), known as "La Avanzadora," was a Venezuelan military leader and national hero during the country's War of Independence from Spain. Born in a small village, she defied traditional gender roles by leading a battalion of women in combat. Ramírez's bravery and strategic insight were pivotal in several key battles, including the Battle of Alto de Los Godos in 1813. Her extraordinary leadership and dedication to Venezuelan independence have made her an enduring symbol of courage and patriotism, celebrated for her contributions to her nation's freedom.

Robert Smalls

Robert Smalls (1839-1915) was an African American hero, politician, and formerly enslaved person whose daring escape to freedom became legendary. Born into slavery in South Carolina, Smalls commandeered a Confederate ship, the Planter, in 1862, sailing it to Union lines and delivering crucial intelligence. His bravery earned him a commission in the Union Navy. After the Civil War, Smalls became a prominent political leader, serving five terms in the U.S. House of Representatives, where he fought for civil rights and public education. Smalls's life exemplifies courage and the relentless pursuit of freedom and equality, making him an enduring figure in American history.

Chesapeake Bay Tower

M.O.M. TEAM LEADERS

Harriet Tubman

**Harriet Tubman (1822-1913) was an iconic African American abolitionist, humanitarian, and Union spy. Born into slavery in Maryland, she escaped to freedom in 1849 and subsequently made 13 missions to rescue approximately 70 enslaved people via the Underground Railroad. Tubman's fearless dedication to liberty extended to her service in the Civil War, where she acted as a scout and spy for the Union Army, leading a successful raid that freed over 700 enslaved people. After the war, she continued to fight for women's suffrage. Tubman's legacy as "Moses" of her people endures, symbolizing relentless courage and the enduring fight for freedom and equality.

Sojourner Truth

Sojourner Truth (1797-1883) was a formidable African American abolitionist and women's rights activist. Born into slavery in New York, she gained her freedom in 1826 and became a powerful orator. Truth's "Ain't I a Woman?" speech, delivered at the 1851 Women's Rights Convention, is celebrated for its poignant demand for equal rights for all women. She tirelessly campaigned against slavery and for women's suffrage, using her unique blend of wit and wisdom.
Truth's life and work have indelibly impacted the fight for social justice, embodying the power of voice and the quest for equality.

ENCOUNTER EXODUS TEAM LEADERS

Charles Sumner

Charles Sumner (1811-1874) was a prominent American statesman and abolitionist known for his fierce advocacy for civil rights. As a U.S. Senator from Massachusetts, Sumner was a leading voice against slavery and a key figure in the Radical Republican movement during Reconstruction.
His passionate speeches, including his famous "Crime Against Kansas" address and his work to promote equal rights for formerly enslaved people, often put him at odds with pro-slavery forces. Sumner's unwavering commitment to justice and equality made him a pivotal figure in the fight for civil rights and social reform.

Thaddeus Stevens

Thaddeus Stevens (1792-1868) was an influential American member of Congress and leader of the Radical Republicans during the Civil War and Reconstruction. A staunch abolitionist, Stevens championed the 13th Amendment to abolish slavery and fought for the rights of formerly enslaved people. His influential role was in drafting and passing Reconstruction legislation to secure civil rights and equality for African Americans. Stevens's fierce advocacy for justice and equality left an indelible mark on American history, shaping the nation's efforts toward civil rights.

John Bingham

John Bingham (1815-1900) was a distinguished American lawyer, politician, and principal framer of the 14th Amendment to the U.S. Constitution. Born in Pennsylvania, Bingham served as a U.S. Congressman from Ohio and played a key role in the impeachment trial of President Andrew Johnson.
His most significant contribution was drafting the 14th Amendment, which established equal protection under the law and due process, fundamentally shaping American civil rights. Bingham's legal understanding and commitment to justice profoundly influenced the nation's legal framework, securing his legacy as a champion of equality and constitutional law.

Don Pio de Jesus Pico IV

Don Pio de Jesus Pico IV (1801-1894) was a prominent Californio politician and the last governor of Alta California under Mexican rule. Born into a mixed-race family in San Gabriel, California, Pico rose to significant political influence, serving as governor in 1832 and from 1845 to 1846.
His tenure was marked by efforts to secularize the missions and redistribute their lands. After the U.S. took control of California, Pico remained an influential figure, advocating for the rights of Californios amidst a rapidly changing society. His life reflects the complex transitions of California from Mexican to American governance, and his legacy endures as a symbol of the state's multicultural heritage.

David Ruggles

David Ruggles (1810-1849) was a pioneering African American abolitionist, journalist, and advocate for the Underground Railroad. Born free in Connecticut, he moved to New York City and became a crucial figure in the anti-slavery movement. Ruggles operated a boarding house for fugitive slaves and published the first African American magazine, *The Mirror of Liberty*
He famously assisted Frederick Douglass in his escape to freedom.
Ruggles's relentless activism and his role in establishing the New York Committee of Vigilance to protect fugitive slaves highlight his significant contributions to the abolitionist cause. His legacy is bravery, dedication, and unwavering commitment to justice and human rights.

E PLURIBUS UNUM
XVI XXXVI XLIV
EQUAL VALUE FOR EVERY LIFE

EARTH – 30,000 YEARS IN THE FUTURE

M.O.M. – MOTHERS of MAN

-Leaders of what was once the United States of America, now "America".

America consists of five regions, each governed by M.O.M.

In 3050, our responses to a series of catastrophic events resulted in all 56 states voting to

dissolve their charter, ratify a new constitution, and approve the M.O.M. regional

structure and the new American flag. Our species has evolved exponentially since then

Now, there is a shared vision of America. Finally, our values match the words in

AMERICA'S NEW LIVING CONSTITUTION.

AND

EARTH IS A FOUNDING MEMBER OF THE UNIVERSE OF NATIONS TO DEFEAT

A CHALLENGE BEYOND COMPREHENSION

E PLURIBUS UNUM